About The California Dashwoods

Make a new future. Choose your true family. Know your own heart.

When Elliott Dashwood's father dies, leaving his family virtually penniless, it's up to Elliott to do what he's always done: be the responsible one. Now isn't the right time for any added complications. So what the hell is he doing hooking up with Ned Ferrars? It's just a fling, right?

Elliott tries to put it behind him when the family makes a fresh start in California, and if he secretly hopes to hear from Ned again, nobody else needs to know. While his mom is slowly coming to terms with her grief, teenage Greta is more vulnerable than she's letting on, and Marianne—romantic, reckless Marianne—seems determined to throw herself headfirst into a risky love affair. And when Elliott discovers the secret Ned's been keeping, he realizes that Marianne isn't the only one pinning her hopes on a fantasy.

All the Dashwoods can tell you that feelings are messy and heartbreak hurts. But Elliott has to figure out if he can stop being the sensible one for once, and if he's willing to risk his heart on his own romance.

Riptide Publishing
PO Box 1537
Burnsville, NC 28714
www.riptidepublishing.com

The California Dashwoods

Cover art: Natasha Snow, natashasnowdesigns.com
Editor: Sarah Lyons
Layout: L.C. Chase, lcchase.com/design.htm

ISBN: 978-1-62649-803-7

First edition
May, 2018

Also available in ebook:
ISBN: 978-1-62649-802-0

The California Dashwoods

by Lisa Henry

RIPTIDE
PUBLISHING

Table of Contents

CHAPTER 1

His father's hand was weightless. Elliott held it gently, rubbing his thumb over the loose, wrinkled skin of his knuckles. His father's fingers were thin and fragile now, and scrubbed clean. Elliott had never seen his father's fingers without paint under his nails.

"Elliott," Henry Dashwood whispered, and Elliott lifted his blurry gaze. The smile on his father's face was almost beatific, but that was probably down to the morphine.

"I'm here." he said, his throat aching. "John's here too, Dad."

John Dashwood was seated on the other side of the bed, his hands folded in his lap. His jaw was clenched tight, and his gaze was fixed on some point just above Henry's pillow.

Henry lifted his free hand and held it out toward John. John looked startled for a moment, and then reached out and took it gently.

"My boys," Henry murmured. "My sons."

They sat for a long moment as Henry drifted off into a doze, only the sound of his heart monitor punctuating the silence.

Elliott didn't even realize Henry was awake again until he spoke.

"John," he said. "John, promise me that you'll look after your brother and your sisters."

John seemed to recoil for a moment, and then he wet his lower lip with his tongue. "I will, Dad." He met Elliott's gaze and then looked down at their father again. "I promise."

"Is Abby coming?" Henry asked, his voice faint.

"Mom's on her way, Dad," Elliott said. "She's on her way with the girls."

Henry passed away before they arrived.

***

Francesca Dashwood, John's wife, arrived the day after Henry passed away. She organized the entire funeral, shoving Abby and her children aside as though Henry's second marriage had been nothing more than a footnote in the Dashwood Family history. Norland Park was filled with a curious mix of mourners, well-wishers, and gawkers. Elliott, Abby, and Marianne suffered their attention, or lack thereof, with varying degrees of politeness. Greta, thirteen years old, locked herself in her bedroom and threatened to stab anyone who tried to drag her out again.

Three days after the funeral, the Naked Blue Lady vanished from her place above the fireplace, and that was when Elliott knew for certain that Francesca had made her move.

The Dashwood Family—always a capital F in Elliott's mind, to distinguish it from the tiny offshoot that he considered actual family—had never forgiven Henry for running off with the help— Abby—and proceeding to prove their dire predictions wrong by living in wedded bliss with her for over twenty years before the cancer took him. Abby had never been interested in the Dashwood Family money. She'd signed the pre-nup the Family lawyers had asked her to. In exchange, the Family had allowed Henry to retain Norland Park, and had provided him with a monthly allowance. Both the house and the allowance had only been guaranteed for as long as Henry lived.

And now, staring at the blank space above the fireplace where the Naked Blue Lady had hung, Elliott knew that he and his mother and his sisters were next.

"She's evil," Marianne announced. "She's a horrible evil troll, and we should let Greta stab her."

"She's not *evil*," Elliott began, and caught Marianne's look. "Okay, so maybe she's a little bit evil, but she's also John's wife, so can we try and be civil, please? Also, why does every scenario that anyone in this family comes up with always involve Greta stabbing someone?"

"Not *every* scenario," Marianne said, her slight smile vanishing as she looked at the blank space above the fireplace. "Mom is going to be pissed."

Right on cue, the French doors flung wide open and Abby Dashwood swept through in one of her trademark kaftans. She stopped when she reached the fireplace, and pressed a hand over her heart. "That *bitch*! Where's my painting?"

Elliott exchanged a glance with Marianne, and together they stepped forward and put their arms around their mother.

"I'm fine!" Abby shook them off. "It's *fine*!"

It clearly wasn't fine. Their wonderful, vibrant mother had been badly shaken by their father's death. She had never once allowed herself to believe that Henry wouldn't go into remission.

"You have to think positive," she'd said a thousand times, and thought so positively herself that she had refused to even begin to entertain any thoughts to the contrary. "Positive thoughts are positive energy, and that's what your father needs right now."

Elliott wasn't certain she'd actually come to terms with the fact that he was gone. Even though they'd all sat in the front row at the funeral, the Family on the left side of the chapel, and Abby and her children on the right side. And poor John, constantly darting between both factions like some frazzled emissary, silently begging Elliott to please prevent Abby or the girls from making a scene.

"Mom," Elliott said now. "Come upstairs."

"Yes," Abby said, and lifted her chin. "Yes, let's go upstairs and pack our bags! I'm not staying in this house a minute longer!" She raised her voice for the benefit of any eavesdroppers. "We're clearly not welcome here!"

Marianne met Elliott's gaze.

"Mom," Elliott said, "we don't have anywhere else to go. We can't just leave."

"Oh, honey." Abby smiled at him, her eyes shining with tears. She reached up and cradled his cheeks in her palms. "Of course we can! All we need is each other."

And somewhere to stay. And jobs. And money for college for Marianne and school for Greta. And health insurance. And a million other things that their father's savings would barely begin to cover. But Elliott didn't have the heart to say any of that.

"We can't go anywhere yet, Mom," he said. "Not without a plan."

"Oh, honey," Abby said again, her smile softening. "You worry too much."

Marianne twined her fingers through Abby's and tugged her

gently toward the stairs. "Come on, Mom. Let's go and see if Greta's stabbed anyone yet."

Elliott watched them go, and then headed down the hallway toward his father's study.

Norland Park, outside of Provincetown, was the only home Elliott had ever known. It had seven bedrooms, a sunroom, and a large parlor that Henry had used as a studio. The house had been built in 1910 in the American Craftsman style, and purchased by the Dashwoods a little over a decade later when Alexander Dashwood made his first million in the burgeoning aeronautics industry. It had served as a summer house for the Family for generations. And now they clearly wanted it back.

Henry Dashwood's study was on the ground floor beside his studio. The hallway smelled of his oil paints. Tears pricked Elliott's eyes, and he wiped them away before he opened the study door.

John was sitting at Henry's desk, flicking through paperwork. He looked up.

"Elliott," he said, his expression suddenly guarded. "Is everything okay?"

"Mom's pretty upset," Elliott said. "The, um, the painting?"

John had the decency to look abashed. "Francesca felt it was *confronting.*"

A wave of grief rose up in Elliott. He could almost hear Henry's vice. *"Art is supposed to be confronting, Elliott. It's supposed to make you uncomfortable! It's supposed to challenge you, to shake you up, to make you feel!"*

Which were all good points, but Elliott still didn't feel he could invite his friends over with the Naked Blue Lady hanging over the fireplace. She was very, very blue, and she was very, very naked. She was also his mom. Elliott had been twelve at the time, and not sure how to explain to his friends that yes, that was his mother sitting spread-legged on that chair, and yes, that was her vulva.

"It meant a lot to them," he said.

John's mouth pressed into a thin line.

And yeah, the painting meant a lot to John too, didn't it? It represented the moment that his father had walked out of his life and away from all his responsibilities to be with the college student he'd hired to be John's *au pair* for the summer. John wasn't a bad guy, but he was never going to be able to put that betrayal aside. Elliott couldn't blame him. Henry had been a wonderful father to Elliott and Marianne and Greta. They'd stolen that from John, in a way.

"There's a little over ten thousand dollars in Dad's savings account," John said at last.

Elliott nodded. "It's what he'd been putting aside, except there's not even enough for Greta's school fees, let alone Marianne's college tuition."

From the moment Henry had been diagnosed, he'd saved what he could from his monthly payments from the Dashwood family trust, but in the end it had been too little, too late. In the end he'd gone so quickly, and there were funeral costs, and taxes, and bills for the alternative treatments they'd tried when it was clear the chemo wasn't working that the insurance hadn't covered.

John sighed. "Elliott, I promised Dad I'd do what I could to help, but most of my assets are tied up in the corporation, or held in trust. I mean, the board isn't going to . . ." He cleared his throat.

Elliott nodded, his eyes stinging again.

"I'll see what I can do," John said. "But Francesca wants the house."

Elliott nodded again, and slipped outside before John could see him crying.

***

Greta's bedroom overlooked the front entrance of Norland Park, and she'd taken to leaning out of her window like a particularly malevolent gargoyle and glaring at anyone who came or went. She was a pretty girl, usually, when she wasn't plotting murder behind the curtain of her dark hair, but Elliott couldn't blame her.

"Oh my god," She exclaimed. "There's another car coming, Elliott! *Another* one!"

Elliott couldn't bring himself to care enough to climb off her bed and go and see.

"It's like Francesca can't even wait until she kicks us out to start filling the place with her awful friends! These ones are driving an Audi." She leaned further out the window.

"Greta!" Elliott leapt off the bed and crossed to the window before she dived out of it. He wrapped an arm around her and looked down.

The black Audi was parked close to the front entrance of the house, and the two young men climbing out were both wearing blazers, khakis and boat shoes.

"Oh, look! It's the Brooks Brothers!" Greta exclaimed.

Greta had no volume control.

Both of the young men looked up.

Elliott and Greta both pushed back from the window at the same time, and landed in a heap on the bedroom floor.

Greta looked at Elliott wide-eyed, and he stared back.

Then, for the first time in what felt like weeks, they both started to laugh.

***

The Brooks Brothers, Elliott learned at dinner, were actually the Ferrars brothers. They were Francesca's younger brothers, Ned and Robert, and they apparently did something in construction. By the looks of them, nothing at the dirty end of that business. The Ferrars family resemblance was clear. The brothers were both tall, blond, and good-looking in a way that had just as much to do with presentation as it did with genetics. Skincare lotions and hair products and designer clothing gave a glossy shine to the brothers' otherwise ordinary exteriors. Elliott found himself glancing at Ned's profile more than once during dinner. His nose was a little long for his face. His jaw was a little wonky. His ears stuck out a bit. Without that two hundred dollar haircut working for him, would he still be as handsome, or would the slightly awkward way he held himself be even more apparent?

Elliott had never had a two hundred dollar haircut in his life. His father might have grown up obscenely wealthy, but his mother hadn't. Two hundred dollars for a haircut when there was a perfectly good pair of scissors lying around? Not on Abby's watch. Even now Elliott's dark hair was tousled and unruly. When it was wet after the shower it hung in tendrils in his eyes and down the back of his neck. When it was dry he rubbed some wax through it, stood it on end, and let it do whatever the hell it wanted for the rest of the day.

And he was the *most* presentable of his side of the family. He'd heard Francesca telling Robert exactly that after the brothers had arrived, before conceding that he was also "the least objectionable."

Not exactly high praise, then.

Elliott glanced at Ned again, and this time Ned caught his gaze and offered him a small smile. Elliott smiled back, a little embarrassed to have been seen looking, and stabbed a piece of carrot.

Dinner with the Family was an ordeal. And Elliott meant that in the most ancient judicial sense. At this point he would rather choose ordeal by fire, and walk over red-hot ploughshares, than endure another round of stilted conversation and barely-concealed barbs. In addition to John and Francesca and the Ferrars brothers, Great Uncle Montgomery had been in residence since the funeral. He hadn't done much except wander around Norland Park poking his cane into the wainscoting and announcing the presence of dry rot, then making grumbled threats to sue Abby for failing to keep the house maintained while she was a tenant.

A *tenant*.

Aunt Cynthia and her husband Aldous had also been staying since the funeral. Elliott couldn't decide if they were better or worse than Montgomery.

"Oh, such pretty children," Aunt Cynthia had said the night she'd arrived. "They don't look anything like Abby, do they?"

Aldous had grunted. "That girl's got metal through her nose."

Worse, probably. They were worse than Montgomery. Montgomery might complain about holes in the wainscoting, but at least he didn't comment on the hole in Marianne's nose.

With the arrival of the Ferrars brothers, it didn't take long for conversation at dinner to turn to the fact that they now had more guests than available guestrooms.

"Well," Francesca said, with a thin smile in Abby's direction, "I'm sure that the children can share, can't they?"

Abby narrowed her gaze. "Excuse me?"

"I think it's only fair to offer guests a proper bedroom, isn't it?" Francesca asked.

Elliott met John's gaze. John looked away.

"*Invited* guests, yes," Abby said. "But I didn't invite them." She grimaced in the direction of Ned and Robert. "No offence."

They both mumbled something that sounded vaguely polite.

"Well, I just thought that Marianne and Greta could share," Francesca pressed on. "That would free up a room."

Abby drew a deep breath. "Excuse you. My daughters don't have to—"

"Ned and Robert can have my room," Elliott said, to head Abby's diatribe off at the pass. Francesca looked smug, John looked relieved, and Abby looked like she had a hell of a lot more to say on the subject. "It's fine. I don't mind."

Ned shot him a worried glance. "That's really not necessary."

"I don't mind," Elliott repeated.

In the awkward silence that settled over the dining room, Great Uncle Montgomery muttered about non-existent mold spores, and Greta turned her steak knife over and over in her palm in a thoughtful way that made Aunt Cynthia shuffle her chair a few inches further away.

Happy families.

***

Elliott went upstairs after dinner to grab some spare clothes and his laptop and phone. He dragged a duffel bag down from the back of his closet and shoved clothes into it. This was his room, but he had known since his father died that he wouldn't be allowed to stay in it. The Family wanted them out of the house. It was a matter of when, not if.

Elliott slid his laptop into his bag, then zipped it up and slung it over his shoulder. He stared down at his rumpled bed, but fuck it. If the Ferrars brothers wanted clean sheets, they could look for them themselves. Elliott crossed to the door and wrenched it open, surprising Ned Ferrars.

He had a suitcase on wheels.

"Sorry," Elliott said, and stepped outside his room.

"No, um, I'm sorry." Ned pressed his lip together. A faint wrinkle appeared at the top of his nose, right between his drawn-together eyebrows. "For, um . . . for your loss, and for everything."

Elliott's heart skipped a beat. He didn't think a single person associated with the Family in any way had stooped to offer him their sympathies. At the funeral, everyone gave their condolences to John, as though Abby and her children, even in that moment, were interlopers with no claim on Henry Dashwood.

He was our dad too.

"Thanks," he murmured, his throat aching.

Ned nodded, and wheeled his little suitcase into Elliott's room. The door snicked shut behind him.

***

Henry's studio was largely undisturbed. It smelled of oil paints and turpentine. Stacks of unfinished canvases leaned against the walls. Elliott set his duffel bag down on the old paint-spattered couch his dad used to take his naps on every afternoon. It still smelled faintly of weed.

He crossed to the wall and traced his shaking fingers down a canvas. The paint was laid on thick, in a choppy texture that read like Braille. He closed his eyes and could hear Henry's voice.

"This is art, my boy! Art! Nothing matters more in the world!"

"Says the man living in a Cape Cod mansion!"

Henry's laughter had filled the room, and then he'd grown uncharacteristically solemn.

"Alexander Dashwood used to fly kites, you know? He used to watch the birds, and fly kites. He wanted to soar. He had an artist's soul as well, I think. What would he make of his descendants, hmm? Making their fortune by manufacturing military drones. All innovators become oppressors, given enough time."

Elliott smiled, his chest aching, and lifted his fingers away from the canvas.

"Love you, Dad," he whispered to the silent studio. "Miss you."

CHAPTER 2

Elliott blinked awake when he heard the rattle of plates. He yawned and stretched, arching his back. "Hey, Mom."

Abby set a mug of tea and a plate of toast down on the old piano stool that Henry had used as a makeshift coffee table. She patted Elliott's legs until he lifted them, and then slid onto the couch. She settled his legs in her lap.

"Why did you sleep down here?" she asked. "You could have shared with one of us."

"You all snore like chainsaws."

Abby snorted and slapped his knee. "All lies!"

Elliott yawned again. "Did you make me breakfast?" He blinked at the toast. "Is that raspberry jam?"

"And lemongrass tea," Abby said. "Your favorites."

"Thanks, Mom." He sat up, and rolled his shoulders until his back cracked. Okay, so the studio couch wasn't the most comfortable place to sleep for an entire night, but he felt close to his dad here. To his dad, and to his entire childhood. Elliott didn't have a single happy memory that he could untangle from the smell of oil paints and turpentine.

He reached out for the tea, and took a sip before he set it back down and selected a small triangle of toast. Abby had cut it into quarters, the way she used to when he was a little kid. He glanced at her, eyebrows raised, and she smiled and knocked her shoulder against his.

"What?" she asked. "You'll always be my baby boy."

The sweet flavor of the raspberry jam burst across his tongue as he bit into the toast.

"And you could use a little looking after," Abby continued, her smile softening from teasing into something tinged with sadness. "Me and your sisters? We can barely be in the same room as those people. It's like pouring gasoline onto the dumpster fire that is your father's family."

Elliott snorted.

Abby leaned against him. "But you're a peacemaker, Elliott. And I don't think I've given you enough credit for that." She wrinkled her nose. "I mean, someone has to deal with the Dashwoods, and I know it can't be me. Thank you for stepping up, baby. And not just now."

Elliott wondered if she was talking about college. Elliott had been two weeks away from graduating high school when Henry was diagnosed. They'd given him eighteen months to two years. He'd made it three years. Sheer stubbornness, probably. Because, as he'd whispered at Elliott one night, there was still so much he had to *do*. He'd painted, and laughed, and danced with Abby, and Elliott's chest had ached when he'd leaned in the doorway and watched them.

Elliott had decided not to go to college, telling himself there would be time for that after. At first he'd meant after his dad got better, but when it had become increasingly clear that wasn't going to happen, and "after" had taken on a darker meaning, Elliott had stayed home to spend time with Henry, and to help schedule his medical appointments, and manage his commissions and the obligations he had to various galleries and collectors. Henry had painted in a frenzy in his last few months.

"They'll be worth a hell of a lot more when I'm dead," he'd declared with a laugh. "Make sure they pay through the nose, Elliott!"

The paintings, and the ten thousand dollars, were all they had left to provide for their future. It wasn't much, long term, and Henry's art had never sold for more than a few grand a piece. He'd been a good artist, but never a truly great one. And the world was full of good artists. The one piece that actually touched on something truly transcendent, something truly incredible, Henry had always refused to sell. The Naked Blue Lady. Or, as she was officially titled, *Abigail in Lamplight*.

"Do you remember John?" Abby asked. "Not *John* John. My cousin John."

Elliott sucked jam off his finger. "John in California?"

"He lives in a little town called Barton Lake. He has a store there.

It's where I met your father, actually. He and the Family were there for the summer and they wanted an *au pair* for John. *John* John, not cousin John. I thought, well, I can make more money looking after some spoiled little snot-nosed rich kid brat than I can doing chalk drawings on the pavement, and—" She cut herself off with a laugh. "And the rest is history."

Elliott saw the moment her expression shifted from gentle grief into something sharper. He reached out and caught her hand. "Cousin John?" he prompted.

Abby shook herself. "He emailed me last night. He's got an apartment above his store that he's happy to let us have. And, if we work a few shifts in the store, he'll let us have it rent-free. Utilities only. It's two bedrooms, so it's going to be a squeeze, but we'll find a way to make it work, won't we?"

Four of them in a two bedroom apartment sounded like a disaster, actually. Abby and Marianne, despite being two peas in a pod—or perhaps because of it—locked horns a lot, and Greta was at the age where she needed her own space to storm off to. It wasn't ideal, but it was a hell of a lot better than the prospect of living in the car. And it was a starting point, right? A roof over their heads while they figured out their next move.

"What's the catch?" Elliott asked.

Abby smiled at him and squeezed his hand. "There's no catch, baby. This is what families *do*." She raised her eyebrows. "Well, families that aren't the Dashwoods."

Elliott quirked his mouth in a wry smile.

That was certainly true. The Dashwood Family was less like a family and more like a corporation. He wondered what Alexander Dashwood, flying his kites and dreaming his dreams, would have thought about the true legacy he'd left. A legacy of lawyers at every family gathering, of board meetings instead of birthdays, and looping signatures on contracts instead of Christmas cards. A legacy of scheming sycophants who relied on the family trust for the income, and spent their lives cozying up to the trustees—Cynthia and Great Uncle Montgomery among them—to keep the money coming.

The Dashwoods really were so awful that it was as easy to reject them on an emotional level as it was to be rejected by them. Practically though . . . well, enough money to get the girls through school and college would be nice. Elliott just needed to convince John to make that happen somehow. John was under no legal obligation—the Family lawyers had made sure that Abby and her children were in line for absolutely nothing—but John wasn't as bad as the rest of them. John was their brother. Except there was also no guarantee that John would have any influence with the rest of the Family.

Elliott thought of the space above the fireplace where the Naked Blue Lady had hung.

"California might be nice," he said at last, when what he really meant was that California might be necessary.

Abby smiled and squeezed his hand again.

***

Elliott took a walk before lunch, his phone in his hand. He needed to escape the house for a while. To escape the narrow looks of Francesca and the Family, and the increasingly furtive, guilty glances that John threw him that did not speak optimistically of their chances of ongoing financial support.

The day was overcast and cool, and the gardens were richly verdant. The damp air smelled of loam and petrichor. Elliott headed for the greenhouse in the center of what had once been a croquet lawn. He'd spent hours here as a child, helping Abby plant out beans and lettuce and tomatoes and peppers. Once, stepping inside the greenhouse had been like stepping into another world, warm and bursting with color even when outside everything was cold and gray. There was none of that today though. Every since Henry had gotten worse, ever since it'd become clear that he wasn't going to beat the disease, the plants in the greenhouse hadn't been tended.

The peppers had taken over. The beans and lettuce were gone. There were one or two straggling tomato plants still hanging on, but they were thin and wilted. Elliott didn't bother to water them. He couldn't imagine that Francesca would want a greenhouse on her croquet lawn. He couldn't imagine her playing croquet either—that might involve putting her cocktail down—but she seemed like the sort of person who would enjoy telling others she had a croquet lawn.

Elliott moved between the rows of raised garden beds. He reached the end of a row, and used his t-shirt to wipe a clear patch on the glass, cleaning it enough to let a little light in. He could see the house from here. It looked blurry and unreal through the smeared glass panes. It even seemed to shimmer a little, like a mirage of a floating city on the horizon, and Elliott felt a sudden hot twist of bitterness for being unable to hold onto the house. He felt bitterness toward John too, for not standing up to the rest of the Dashwoods even though he was better than them. And for his parents, for not planning for this, for not thinking the worst could happen—that Henry might die so young, without having time to set aside enough money to provide for his family. Of course the worst could happen. The worst happened to people every f.cking day.

He closed his stinging eyes and exhaled slowly.

"Oh! I'm so sorry!"

Elliott spun around, damp earth and dead leaves crunching under his shoe. Ned Ferrars was standing in the entrance to the greenhouse, a pair of imported beer bottles nestled in the crook of his elbow.

"I didn't know anyone was in here," Ned said, color rising in his face. "I'll, um. I'll just . . ."

"Are you sneaking out here to day drink?" Elliott asked, warming to that idea immensely. "I won't tell if you share."

Ned looked uncertain for a moment, and then flashed him a bashful smile He stepped forward and passed Elliott a beer. "It'll be our secret then."

Elliott sat on the edge of a garden bed, and gestured at the space beside him. He watched as Ned sat too, and then twisted the top off the beer. "When I was six I ran away from home." He took a swig of the beer. "I made it this far."

"That's, um, disappointing?"

Elliott shrugged. "I just wanted to sleep with the carrots."

Ned cocked an eyebrow. "Worst tagline for a mafia movie ever."

Elliott almost sprayed a mouthful of beer over himself. He swallowed with difficulty while the laugh tried to escape him, and wiped his mouth with the back of his hand. "Holy shit! Seriously?"

Ned's smile was the most genuine one Elliott had seen from him.

"Wow." Elliott took another sip of beer, more carefully this time just in case Ned had more terrible jokes up his sleeve. "That was truly terrible. Thank you. I needed a good laugh."

Ned reached out and clinked their beer bottles together. "Then I'm glad I could help."

"Death is weird," Elliott said, and then winced. "Sorry. You came to get quietly buzzed, right? Not to sign up to whatever's going on inside my head right now."

Ned's expression was soft and warm. "I've been told I'm an okay listener."

Elliott exhaled slowly. "We knew this was coming for months. I mean, for years it was a possibility, but for months we've known for sure. And yet somehow it's still shocking. Somehow my brain still can't wrap itself around the fact that Dad's gone. That he's dead. That I was at his funeral the other day. His *funeral*." He shook his head. "Weird."

Ned took a sip of beer.

"I hate to think what you've been told about him." Elliott dragged the toe of his shoe through the dirt. "But he was a good dad to us. Maybe not so much to John, but he was to us. He was always so full of life. Always doing crazy, wild things. I mean, how can he just not be here anymore? That makes no sense. I know he's gone. I *know* it. I just don't know how I'm supposed to deal with it."

"Time," Ned said at last, his voice low. "That's a shitty answer, I know, but it's the only one I've got. Just time."

"Yeah." Elliott nodded. "I just go from feeling numb, to getting these weird bursts of energy like I should be *doing* something, except there's nothing I can do, and this whole shitfight with the Family makes everything a hundred times more fucked up." He shot Ned a guilty look. "Sorry. I don't mean . . ."

Ned shrugged and quirked his mouth in a smile. "My sister thinks your mother is a gold digger. That's not a secret."

"Twenty-two years of marriage," Elliott said. "I guess she was playing the long con."

"I guess she was." Ned's smile faded. "Francesca's close with John's mother, and John's mother doesn't have a high opinion of your mother. Francesca has very much taken that onboard. But I'm not here to take sides or to run to Francesca with whatever you tell me. I know when to keep my mouth shut, Elliott."

Elliott bit his bottom lip, anxiety battling with some new emotion. Something needy and hot and guilty. Something *alive*. "Yeah?"

Ned's gaze dropped to Elliott's mouth. "Yes."

Elliott wedged his beer bottle in the garden bed beside him and twisted his body toward Ned's. If Ned was surprised, he gave no sign of it. He met Elliott halfway, dragging his fingers through his hair and angling their mouths together. Ned tasted like beer, and Elliott chased the bitter flavor with his tongue. He felt more alive than he had in days, in *months*. He felt the blood rushing to his dick, and hardened in his jeans.

It was good. So good. For so long he'd been walking underwater, sluggish, deaf, slow and mute, and finally he could *feel* something again. Finally he had sharp-edged sensation to chase down. He was back in his body at last, and he *wanted*. The rush of sensation left him breathless, panting against Ned's mouth. His skin tingled, and he felt more buzzed than his few mouthfuls of beer warranted.

"I don't do this," he whispered.

Ned's lips moved against his as he spoke. "Me neither. *God*."

Elliott felt as though he had blood pumping in his veins for the first time in longer than he could remember. He was no numb observer, trapped behind a pane of thick grimy glass. This was life, and he was a part of it again. He wanted to dig his fingers into the dirt and feel it.

He dug his fingers into Ned's shirt instead, twisting the fabric in his grasp as they kissed again.

There was a sudden dull thump, and Ned jerked away and then leapt to his feet. His jeans were soaked with beer, and he reached down to right the offending bottle. "Sorry. Shit. *Sorry*."

"It's okay," Elliott said, his face burning. He wanted to laugh at Ned's embarrassment, and at his own. Who knew how much further they might have gone if Ned hadn't knocked his beer over? Whatever weird spell had taken hold of both of them, Ned had broken it with his clumsiness, and then they were just two awkward guys again, avoiding eye contact in a greenhouse that smelled of damp earth and fertilizer.

They parted with mumbled words and flushed skin, and Elliott headed back to the house. A soft pattering of rain, more like mist, shrouded the garden. It was cold on his skin, and he relished it. He entered the house through the kitchen door, and managed to avoid any of the Family as he crept upstairs. He ignored the STAY OUT!!!! sign on Greta's door, and slipped inside to find her and Marianne lying together on the bed, sharing a pair of earbuds as they listened to some song on Greta's phone. They shuffled over when they saw Elliott, and he lay down beside Greta, his clothes damp.

Greta patted his side. "Mom's gone into town. She said if you want anything, text her."

"I don't need anything."

"She's getting boxes," Greta said. "For the *move*."

She drew the word out like it was ominous.

"We don't know anything for sure yet," Elliott said.

Marianne wrinkled her nose, and the light caught on her nose ring. She tugged her earbud out. "We know we're not staying here."

"California is a long way away," Greta said, scowling at the ceiling.

"I think it'll be good," Marianne said decisively. "It'll be an adventure! We'll meet new people, and do new things, and never have to deal with Dad's asshole family again, and it'll be *amazing*."

Sometimes Elliott envied Marianne's optimism. Sometimes he secretly scorned her naivety. She was his best friend, but they were complete opposites. They balanced each other out, he supposed, contrary and complementary at the same time: yin and yang. Elliott had always been the realist, and Marianne the idealist. Which actually made Elliott the odd one out in their family.

Henry and Abby had always encouraged their children to be free spirited, to be whatever they wanted to be, to relish the journey just as much as the destination, but it wasn't that easy anymore. It had been so far because they'd had Norland Park and they'd had Henry's monthly check from the Dashwoods, supplemented by what he made with his art, that had covered living expenses and school fees and health insurance, but now those things were gone . . . Elliott worried that his sisters had no real idea of what it might be like without any money. Their freedom was a very specific sort of freedom: it was white, and it was wealthy, and it was privileged in a way they'd never had to dissect. They'd never had to struggle.

Abby said he worried too much, but someone had to.

Greta squirmed. "Why are you wet?"

"I was in the garden. I went to the greenhouse."

There must have been something in his tone, because Marianne raised herself up onto an elbow and gave him a look like she knew he wasn't telling the whole story.

Elliott reached for the earbud Marianne had discarded and jabbed it into Greta's free ear. She squealed and tried to bite him.

"I kissed Ned," he said, one hand splayed on Greta's sternum to keep her more or less subdued.

"Ned?" Marianne's jaw dropped.

"Ned?" Greta echoed. She tugged the earbuds free. "My music was off, doofus."

"Why?" Marianne asked, her forehead wrinkling. "I mean, that's not the sort of thing you do, Elliott."

Elliott sighed. "I don't know."

"He's nice," Greta said. "Like, I think Francesca bathes in the blood of virgins as part of her skincare routine or whatever, and Robert just kind of takes up space, doesn't he? I don't think he even has a personality. But Ned actually seems to be nice."

Marianne shrugged. "He kind of does."

"He was probably adopted," Greta said in a stage whisper.

Elliott snorted and elbowed her, and she thwapped him in the side of the head with her earbuds.

"I think it's wonderful." Marianne smiled brightly, and Elliott knew she was plotting out some grand romance. He and his sisters had been raised on their parents' love story: Love was a force of nature that nobody could withstand. It was a crashing storm that broke over two people, and all they could do was cling together and let the rushing water carry them away. Love was indomitable. It made the world.

Marianne was waiting to dive breathlessly into her own epic love story—potential heartbreak be damned—and now her eyes shone with the idea that Elliott might want to do the same. "You should do something romantic! We could get some candles for the studio, and you could have a picnic dinner in there!"

"Oh, Jesus! *No!*" Elliott almost laughed, the idea was so absurd. "I made out with a guy, Mar, I didn't trip and fall into a fairytale!"

"Elliott!" Marianne looked aghast. "Maybe it could be something special!"

"And maybe it's just a thing," Elliott shot back.

In the sudden silence, Marianne narrowed her eyes at Elliott. Not accusative, but speculative, as though she thought there was something he wasn't saying. If there was, it was a mystery to Elliott as well. There weren't any words he was holding back intentionally, but there was a vague, unfamiliar sense of *something* when he thought of the kiss. He couldn't put a name to it, and whatever it was, it was too vague and nebulous to go building fantasies on.

Elliott closed his eyes briefly and sighed. "It was just a thing."

He replayed the sensation of Ned's mouth on his, of his tongue sliding against Elliott's, of his fingers tugging in Elliott's hair. Of the shivers of heat and pleasure that ran through his body in a series of diminishing tremors like the aftershocks of some seismic event. Ned's kiss had been incredible. It had awakened the parts of Elliott that stress and grief and tiredness had forced down. But it wasn't love. It was attraction.

Elliott didn't even know Ned, and that was fine.

Not everything was a Technicolor extravaganza, and that was fine too. It was all right to find small joys in small moments. It was all right to have small dreams. There was a comfort in those that his mother and sisters would never understand. That his father never had. It was all right.

He opened his eyes again and stared up at Greta's bedroom ceiling.

Greta clicked her tongue and turned her head toward Marianne. "Elliott was probably adopted too," she said at last.

CHAPTER 3

It was dark.

Elliott shuffled down the hallway, drawn by the clattering of pans, and leaned in the kitchen doorway. He was still mostly asleep, yawning and blinking and just alert enough to realize how very weird this was.

Ned Ferrars, wearing a pair of soft-looking flannel pajama pants and a rumpled shirt, was cracking eggs in a bowl. His brow was furrowed in concentration, and he stopped every few moments to show his progress to Greta.

Greta was also in her pajamas. Most of her hair was bundled up under a knitted cap, but a few tendrils escaped to hang down the back of her pink Hello Kitty shirt. Greta swore she wore it ironically, but Elliott wasn't so sure. Greta was wielding a wooden spoon in one hand, and a carton of milk in the other.

There was a bag of flour sitting on the counter, a tub of butter beside it, and a frying pan on the stovetop.

"Like this?" Ned asked, showing Greta the bowl.

"You've never actually beaten an egg in your life, have you?" she asked him. "It's supposed to be all even and the same color. Not like whatever you've got going on there. That looks like a science experiment, not cooking."

Elliott laughed quietly.

Ned turned around. His expensive haircut was mussed up. A flush rose on his face. "Elliott, hi."

"We're making pancakes," Greta said. "Wanna help?"

Elliott shuffled into the kitchen. "What time is it?"

"Two o'clock," Greta said.

"In the morning?"

"No, in the afternoon, doofus." Greta narrowed her eyes at him.

"What do you think?"

Elliott yawned again. "I think I want some pancakes."

Ned smiled at him, and Elliott wasn't sure how much to read into that. It seemed like the sort of smile that spoke of kindness, of shyness, and of moments of time in the middle of the night when the usual rules didn't apply. Elliott fought the sleepy urge to close the distance between them. To tuck himself against Ned's side and just be close and comfortable. In the middle of the night, in Elliott's still-dreaming brain, it was allowed to be that simple.

He liked Ned.

He liked his not-quite-handsome features. He liked the way he looked a little awkward even now, as though he was never quite sure how to hold himself. He liked the way he knew that he was gentle and thoughtful underneath that. And even in his sleep-addled state, a warmth flooded through Elliott's core as he thought of their kiss, and of the strange desperation that had seized him in that moment. To be close to someone. To be wanted. To be reckless and alive.

Greta took the bowl off Ned and set it on the counter. "Now put in the flour and the milk and the butter," she said.

"How much?" Ned asked.

"How have you never made pancakes?" Greta made a face, her nose wrinkling. "You just . . . you just tip them in until it looks right."

Ned shrugged. "I have no idea what looks right."

"Here." Elliott peeled himself off the doorjamb and stepped inside the kitchen. He brushed against Ned as he moved up to the counter. Their shoulders knocked together. He reached for the flour. "You're not allowed to call it a family tradition until you can make it without a recipe."

"Is that so?" Ned watched as he opened the flour.

"Dad could make gingerbread without looking at a recipe," Greta said. "Even though there's only like a two week period in December when it's appropriate to make gingerbread."

"Luckily we don't stand much on 'appropriate' in this family," Elliott murmured, tipping some flour into the eggs.

"So you're a family that makes pancakes in the middle of the night." Ned nodded. "I can get behind that."

"Says the guy who can't even beat an egg," Greta pointed out.

"Excuse you, I'm on a learning curve."

Greta snorted, and lifted the bowl. She held it in the crook of her arm and began to stir the ingredients with the wooden spoon.

"Aren't you supposed to use a mixer?" Ned asked her.

Greta leveled a stare at him. "This spoon is a mixer. See how I'm using it to mix these things?"

Ned tilted his head. "You are incredibly sarcastic, aren't you?"

Greta grinned. "Thank you!"

Elliott yawned again, and Ned knocked him gently with his shoulder. The gesture was so small, so affectionate, that Elliott's heart skipped a beat. He wanted to reach up and card his fingers through Ned's messy hair. He wanted to grip it, and angle Ned's face toward his for a kiss.

Instead he moved away. He checked the progress of the pancake batter as Greta stirred it furiously with the wooden spoon, and then moved to the stove. He turned one of the burners on.

It didn't take long for Greta to get the batter ready, and Elliott found himself in charge of cooking the pancakes. It was mostly a mess. The batter was too thin, so the pancakes came out more like crepes, but Greta declared them a success anyway. She spread a layer of butter over the first one, which melted immediately, and then sprinkled sugar on it before rolling it up.

"This doesn't look like a pancake," Ned challenged when she offered him one.

"Shut up and try it. It's nice."

Ned took a bite of the pancake. A drop of melted sugar and butter slid down his chin.

"Shit," he said, holding the dripping pancake in one hand and wiping at his chin with the thumb of his other hand. "This is really good."

A splat of sugary butter hit the floor.

"Shit," Ned said again, and moved to stand over the sink.

"Amateur." Greta curved the end of her pancake up so it didn't drip as she ate it.

Elliott ate the third pancake hot from the pan, and gave the next one to Ned. Greta was yawning by the time she finished her second. By her third she could barely keep her eyes open anymore.

"I'm going to bed," she mumbled, and shuffled out of the kitchen.

There was still enough batter in the bowl for one last pancake, so Elliott tipped it into the pan, and then put the bowl in the sink to rinse it.

"Want the last one?" he asked Ned.

"We can share it."

"Okay." Elliott returned to the stovetop. "What were you guys doing up at this hour anyway?"

"I was in the library looking for something to read, and Greta came in and asked me if I'd ever seen *Assassination Classroom*." Ned shook his head. "And before I know it we're four episodes in, and it's 2 a.m. Have *you* seen it? It's very weird."

"That's the one with the big yellow octopus thing, right? Who blew up the moon?"

"Only seventy percent of the moon," Ned said, and then snorted. "Great. Now that's a thing I apparently know."

"Greta likes to force people to watch that show."

"Why?" Ned asked, raising his eyebrows.

Elliott shrugged. "It's Greta."

He didn't tell Ned that Greta had clearly been testing him, and the fact that she'd make him pancakes meant he'd passed the test. *Assassination Classroom* and pancakes were her seal of approval. She sure as shit hadn't invited Great Uncle Montgomery to watch her weird show with her.

Elliott rolled the last pancake up, and then tore it in two. Sugar and butter ran down his fingers. He passed half the pancake to Ned, and Ned took it, his gaze fixed on Elliott's sticky fingers. Elliott, his heart beating faster, raised those fingers to his mouth and licked them clean.

"I, um . . ." And suddenly Ned was crowding him against the counter, and they were kissing.

It wasn't like their first kiss. It wasn't sweet and gentle. This kiss was all about heat. About chasing the taste of sugar. Elliott dropped his pancake on the floor—because fuck it—and gripped Ned's hips. He tugged him closer, opening his mouth and pressing his tongue against Ned's.

And then Ned was pulling away, eyes wide. "Wait." He put his hands on Elliott's chest. "Wait."

Elliott held his gaze, breathing heavily.

"Wait." Ned's tone was softer now. He lifted his hand and pressed it gently against the side of Elliott's face. "You're not in a good place right now. And I'm . . ." He shook his head as though to clear it. "I don't think this is something we should be doing. Not like this."

Heat rose in Elliott's face. "Oh."

"I like you," Ned said. "I *like* you, but you just buried your father, Elliott."

Elliott suddenly envied the Victorians and their regimented mourning periods. The slow shedding of black clothing for dull shades of gray and lavender. The precision of the entire process. The certainty of it. When was the appropriate time to fold away the black mourning clothes and make out with a guy in the kitchen in the middle of the night?

Elliott snorted out a laugh at the idea of the Victorians ever approving anything like *this*, and Ned looked startled.

Okay, so yes, he wasn't thinking clearly right now.

Ned had a point.

"Yeah," he said, letting his eyes close.

Ned rubbed his thumb gently along Elliott's cheekbone. The soft touch brought Elliott out in goose bumps, and made him wonder again just exactly what he wanted from Ned Ferrars: solace, or sex? Maybe he wanted both, and that was stupid. He didn't even know Ned.

He opened his eyes and searched Ned's gaze. He didn't know what it was he was looking for. He didn't know what it was he found, but he thought he saw the same uncertainly reflected in Ned's eyes.

"Yeah," he said again, softly. He smiled, and edged out from between Ned and the counter. His cheek felt warm from where Ned had been touching it. "I'm going to clean up and go back to bed. Goodnight."

"Goodnight," Ned murmured.

When Elliott looked up again, Ned was gone.

***

"I knew," Henry Dashwood had always said. "I took one look at your mother and I knew."

Elliott took a lot of looks at Ned Ferrars. Quick glances across the dining table. Slower ones when nobody else was watching. Small looks, and small smiles, accompanied each time by a burst of warmth, by a frisson of anticipation, but Elliott didn't *know*. He felt as far away from knowing as was humanly possible, but he liked sharing those hidden smiles with Ned. It felt a little like having a secret ally in an enemy camp, and Elliott could really use that right now.

The Family was terrible, and Abby wasn't helping. She was still upset that Francesca had removed the Naked Blue Lady and was demanding that it be put back. Specifically that Elliott find a way to get Francesca to put it back.

"This is still my house!" she fumed to Elliott, pacing back and forth in her bedroom.

Elliott sat on the end of the bed and watched her.

The room still felt like his dad might walk back in at any minute. His paint-stained clothes still hung in the closet. His watch was lying on the bedside table, on top of a book that still had a bookmark in it.

"Mom," Elliott said. "The painting's fine. It's in the library."

"If she does anything to it . . ." Abby squared her shoulders.

"She's not going to do anything to it, Mom," Elliott said, keeping his tone gentle.

Abby stopped pacing and glared at him, hands on her hips. "And how do you *know* that, Elliott?"

"Mom," Elliott said with a sigh. "Come on."

"Elliott, they're pushing us out of our *home*!" Her voice cracked and her eyes filled with tears.

Elliott stood and moved to embrace her.

This was what their grief was. This was the place it brought them back to every time. To tears and the feeling of the ground crumbling beneath their feet. Elliott was tired of it, and guilty for feeling that way, and his dad's watch was still on the bedside table, and how was any of this even *real*?

He was twenty years old, and he wasn't ready for this.

He closed his eyes as he hugged his mom, and tried to feel stronger than he was.

***

In the afternoon they had a picnic on the overgrown croquet lawn. Abby sat on the blanket with her back to the house, and a half-smile on her face that fell far short of reaching her eyes. Greta sat across from her, craning her head to watch for movement from the house, as though she was expecting the Family to attempt some devious maneuver if she looked away for even a second.

Marianne leaned against Elliott, and he exchanged a glance with her, and saw his own trepidation mirrored there. For all that he and Marianne were very different people, they had always been incredibly close. Elliott couldn't remember a time when Marianne hadn't been at his side. If life was a series of snapshots, then Marianne was in every single one, her brilliant grin a counterpoint to Elliott's shyer smile— and Norland Park was in every frame as well. It wasn't just a house. It was their home, and soon there would be no more picnics on the lawn.

Marianne handed him a peanut butter sandwich.

Picnics were another family tradition. Someone would grab the blanket from the bottom of the kitchen pantry and announce that they were eating outside today. There was nothing as planned as a picnic basket involved. Just sandwiches stacked on a plate, plastic cups, and the jug of cold apple tea from the refrigerator.

Growing up, Elliott had thought it was perfectly normal for families to migrate outside and sit on the grass to eat their lunch. People did it in city parks, didn't they? Why not their own gardens? He hadn't realized for a long time that there was anything odd about it at all. And, when it came to oddness, impromptu picnics were definitely one of his favorite family quirks.

"Someone's watching us from the kitchen," Greta announced, and squinted. "I think it's Uncle Aldous."

Marianne craned her head to see.

Elliott closed his eyes, and concentrated on the feeling of the sun against the back of his neck. He didn't want to talk about the Family. Not right now. He needed a break from them just as much as his mother and his sisters did. He didn't need reminders of them invading their picnic like ants.

He opened his eyes again when Marianne nudged him.

"Remember that time we were playing chasey and you ran headfirst into the greenhouse?" she asked with a smile.

Elliott touched the tiny scar hidden in his hairline reflexively. "I had to get a tetanus shot."

"Well, trust you to run into a nail," Marianne teased.

"I was *six*."

"And couldn't outrun a four-year-old? What a loser."

Elliott laughed.

Abby smiled at them fondly. "I remember when we had to take Greta for a rabies shot because she got bitten by that raccoon."

"That wasn't my fault," Greta said.

"You had a raccoon in your bedroom!" Marianne exclaimed.

"I was domesticating him." Greta shrugged. "It turned out he wasn't really on board with that plan."

Elliott's chest tightened, and that familiar ache rose up in him. Norland Park held so many memories. It was the only home he'd ever known, and he didn't want to leave it. But there was nothing he could do to stop it. The Family had descended like vultures the moment his dad had died, here to pick his bones clean.

What was Norland Park to them but a figure on a spreadsheet courtesy of some valuation by a realtor? It wasn't about money for Elliott, it was about *home*, but what did that word even mean to the Family? Elliott couldn't imagine any of them sitting on the grass reminiscing. And maybe that was unfair. Maybe Great Uncle Montgomery had a favorite chair in a favorite spot. Maybe Cynthia stepped out of her heels at the end of a long day and padded barefoot through her house, soaking it in. Maybe Francesca looked at Norland Park and imagined her future children running through the halls, breathless with laughter.

Then again, why should Elliott feel generously disposed toward any of them?

They sat out on the lawn for a while after the sandwiches were finished. Greta was the first one to head back to the house, carrying the plates and cups. Marianne and Abby were the next to go, leaving Elliott lying on the blanket with his arms folded behind his head.

He dozed, sun blind. He soaked up the light and the warmth, lost in a lifetime of memories.

"Hey."

Elliott jolted awake, unaware he'd even slipped into sleep. He blinked up as the silhouette looming over him transformed itself into Ned.

"Hey," he said, his voice scratchy with sleep.

Ned held up a bottle of beer. "Want one?"

Elliott pushed himself into a seated position. "Thanks."

Ned sat down beside him. He twisted the top off the beer and handed it to Elliott, then took a sip from his own bottle. "You okay?"

"That's a question I really don't know how to answer."

"Short answer, no."

Elliott quirked his mouth in a smile. "No."

"Listen, if there's anything you need me to do, you can ask." Ned looked so earnest that Elliott's heart clenched. "Like, I'm probably totally out of line here, but have you talked to a lawyer?"

Elliott picked at the label on his beer. "Mom doesn't want that. She doesn't want anything to do with them. She thinks going after them would prove them right." He shrugged. "They cut Dad out twenty years ago. It's pretty watertight, from what I understand."

"Have you checked?" Ned asked him in an undertone.

"Their lawyers would crush us. Keep us tied up for years. It's how they operate. It's not worth it. The best we can hope for is that John will come through for money for school and stuff."

Ned looked at him worriedly.

"Montgomery has a daughter, you know?" Elliott said. "Not his wife's. She was the housekeeper's. She must be fifty-something by now. She's never seen a penny, because every time she tried, they just dragged her back into court. Appeal after appeal after appeal. They've probably paid millions to their lawyers because they'd rather pay them than her. You don't win with people like them. You can't."

Ned was silent for a long time. "I'm sorry," he said at last.

"You don't win," Elliott said again.

Ned didn't say anything. He reached out and put his hand over Elliott's where it rested on the blanket. He threaded their fingers together. Quiet, solid comfort.

They sat in silence, and Elliott felt like he could breathe again for the first time in days.

CHAPTER 4

John and Francesca were spending the day antiquing in town, so Elliott didn't get a chance to press John on whether or not he'd be able to give them more financial support than the Family wanted. Elliott wasn't too proud to go cap in hand to his half-brother, and couldn't help but wonder if Francesca was intentionally keeping John away from him. It was starting to feel that way, but maybe Elliott was being unfair. John probably needed a break from the Family too, because Great Uncle Montgomery and Cynthia and Aldous were apparently fixtures in Norland Park nowadays. They'd adopted strategic positions throughout the house that meant only the bedrooms were safe territory to retire to, or, in Elliott's case since he didn't have one of those right now, the studio.

In the afternoon, tired of working through a hundred different and equally depressing scenarios for the future in his head, Elliott gave up and fetched himself a blank canvas from the stack leaning against the far wall. Elliott was no painter, but who was going to use it now? And the canvas was already assembled, primed with gesso, and ready to go.

The studio was too hot to put on one of Henry's paint-stained smocks, so Elliott stripped off his shirt to save ruining it, and left it on the couch. He pushed open the windows to let the cool air inside, turned on the radio to the station Henry had last been listening to, and began to paint. He'd never had the right sort of temperament for painting. He didn't have an artist's soul, and found it difficult to disengage from the everyday and lose himself in the kind of trance-like headspace that Henry had often existed in for days on end.

Elliott had sometimes envied his dad's all-consuming passion for painting, even if he had never really understood it. Art, to him, was a contradictory thing. He couldn't deny how meaningful it was to his parents, and to Marianne and to Greta, but at the same time it was also incredibly meaning*less*. Hours and days lost hunting for truth and beauty and *something* in the ether, the answer always remaining out of reach, exhilarating and frustrating in equal measure. He could see how the pursuit of art was invigorating to some people, was *vital*, but Elliott wasn't made that way. But he had always liked the smell of the oil paints.

He tended to produce abstract pieces. Shapes and lines and blocks of color that pleased his eye and satisfied his urge to cover every piece of the canvas. He'd never been good at human figures, or even landscapes, and his bowls of fruit were terrible. But none of that mattered in Henry's studio. Art was the process, the journey, and not the finished product. Art was about *living*.

A pang of something too sweet to call grief stabbed his heart. He could feel his dad's presence here still. He almost thought that if he glanced up from his canvas he'd see Henry watching him with his proud, gentle smile. He closed his eyes, and laid an arc of cadmium green across the canvas. The placement of the sweeping line didn't matter. Only the faint metallic smell of the paint mattered, and the fact that Elliott had left something on the canvas that had not been there before.

He opened his eyes again and worked for a while to the sound of the radio and the memory of his father's smile. The canvas he had chosen was large. Too large for an easel, so Elliott had learned it up against the wall, against a stack of finished paintings that were protected by a drop sheet. He probably should have chosen a smaller canvas, but what did it matter now? Any that they couldn't sell or store securely before they left would probably be tossed into the nearest dumpster by Francesca.

A faint knock at the door startled Elliott, and he steeled himself. Because it wasn't as though Abby or his sisters would knock. Meaning that it was someone from the Family. Elliott tucked the paintbrush behind his ear, and looked around for a cloth to wipe his fingers on. His hands were speckled with paint, and there were a few smudges on his torso that blended into his skin like bruises.

He turned toward the door, wiping his hands. "Come in!"

The door opened to reveal Ned. He stepped inside the studio cautiously, holding a plate in front of him. "Um, Marianne said I should bring you a snack."

Elliott resisted the urge to roll his eyes at Marianne and her meddling. "Thanks."

Ned closed the distance between them. He set the plate down on the old piano stool, amid the paints and brushes. He stared at Elliott's canvas for a moment. "That's, um . . ." A flush crept up his throat, on the faint pinkish end of the of the quinacridone red spectrum. "I don't know much about art."

"It's shit," Elliott said frankly, smiling at Ned's startled expression. He shrugged. "It's sophomoric and unsophisticated and messy." He reached for the sandwich. "But I enjoyed doing it."

Ned's answering smile was soft. "I think it looks good."

"It looks like the sort of thing you'd buy in a dollar store to decorate your dorm room with," Elliott told him around a mouthful of turkey sandwich. "Goes perfectly with bookshelves made of cinderblocks."

Ned inspected the painting again, his brow furrowed. "I don't think it's quite that bad."

Elliott set the sandwich down, leaving blue fingerprints on the bread. He took the paintbrush from behind his ear and held it out to Ned. "Have a try."

Ned looked from Elliott's face to the paintbrush and then back again. "Are you serious?"

"It's a painting," Elliott said. "Not delicate surgery."

Ned took the paintbrush. His gaze didn't leave Elliott's face. "Um, you have a little. . ." He reached out with his free hand and brushed his fingertips against Elliott's cheek. They came away blue. "I think I just made it worse."

Elliott smiled. His cheek tingled. He stepped into Ned's space, feeling the cold dab of the paintbrush against his skin. He stepped back again, and looked down at the blue stripe it had left on his ribs. His smile widened.

"Shit," Ned whispered. "I'm sorry."

Elliott curled his fingers around Ned's, and, with no idea of exactly what the hell he was doing, drew the paintbrush up his torso. The paint left a line from his sternum to his collarbone. His chest rose and fell heavily.

Hot as hell or stupid as fuck? Elliott wasn't sure he could actually tell.

He met Ned's gaze. Ned's eyes were wide, and there was something in his expression approaching panic. Elliott was just about to blurt out an apology, or make a joke of it, when suddenly Ned was pushing him up against the canvas and leaning in to lick a stripe up the side of his throat.

Paint squished against Elliot's shoulder blades. The paintbrush clattered to the floor.

"Shit," Ned said. His breath was hot against Elliott's neck. "I've ruined your painting."

"It was a terrible painting anyway," Elliott reminded him, and reached for the hem of Ned's shirt, tugging it out of his khakis.

Art is about living, Elliott, his father used to say, and Elliott thought that maybe he'd never been very good at art, but he was getting the hang of this living business. A part of him recognized the total irrationality of this thing with Ned, but it didn't matter. He was allowed to do something just because it made him feel good, made him feel more vibrant than art ever had. He was allowed to pursue whatever this was in the full knowledge that it wasn't the start of anything, like Marianne thought. This was enough, right here.

"Is the paint toxic?" Ned asked, pulling back enough to straighten up and meet Elliott's gaze.

"I mean, if you drank a few gallons of it, probably. This is fine." He laughed as Ned took him at his word and pressed him harder against the canvas.

The muscles in Ned's abdomen—not quite defined enough to be called a six pack—shifted under his skin as Elliott tugged his shirt off and tossed it onto the floor.

"I don't have anything," Ned said.

"S'okay." Elliott jutted out his chin so he could nip the side of Ned's jaw. "Let's just, um . . ." He slid a hand down Ned's abdomen, his fingers leaving streaks of paint down his skin and then the khakis that had probably cost more than anything Elliott had in his closet. He tugged the button free and pulled the zip down. Ned's dick was already bulging against his underwear.

"Yes," Ned said. "Yeah."

Elliott dragged Ned's khakis and underwear down, leaving them in a tangle somewhere around his thighs. Ned reached forward to do the same to Elliott's faded jeans, and then they were rutting against one another, a hand each pressing their dicks together, and one of Elliott's legs hooked behind Ned.

Elliott's breath caught in his throat as he stared down at their dicks. It was ridiculous. Their hands were slick with paint and sweat and pre-cum, and it was the craziest, hottest thing Elliott had ever done. Need coiled tight in his lower belly, and then in his balls, and he hadn't been this hard this fast in years now.

He hadn't been this *alive*.

He dug the fingers of his free hand into Ned's shoulder. Ned rocked with him in the choppy rhythm they'd somehow fallen into. Words were unnecessary. Impossible, maybe. They panted against one another, fixated by the sight of their dicks clenched together in their hands and in the fast-building pleasure they were chasing.

Elliott came first, his bare toes curling as he spurted cum all over their joined hands. Ned followed moments later, hunched over and pressing his forehead against Elliott's shoulder.

Elliott dropped his head back, not giving a fuck in that moment about getting paint in his hair.

"Oh my god," Ned whispered after a moment.

Elliott's lazy, satisfied smile was curtailed by a screeching echo: "*Oh my god!*"

Elliott snapped his eyes open and saw, over Ned's shoulder, Francesca and John standing in the doorway of the studio. John looked dumbfounded. Francesca looked like she was about to transform into a harpy.

"Oh my god!" she screeched again. "You dirty little gold-digging *whore!*"

Elliott stared at her blankly for a moment.

This probably meant they weren't getting the money for Marianne's college or Greta's school fees, right?

Yeah.

Probably.

***

There were sporadic shouting matches up and down the halls of Norland Park for the rest of the afternoon, and once, when Elliott ventured into the kitchen to get a glass of juice, he ran straight into Aunt Cynthia, who looked him up and down and announced that she *knew* it and had known it all along.

"I wouldn't expect anything else from one of *her* children."

"Oh, fuck off, you poisonous old hag," Marianne said from behind Elliott, and then shrugged at his expression. "What? You heard her. They're not going to think any less of us if we finally say what we really think."

Marianne wasn't the only one who figured Elliott's transgression was a good reason to go carte blanche on the Family. He caught Greta releasing a jar full of spiders underneath Great Uncle Montgomery's bedroom door.

Most of Francesca's anger seemed to be directed, surprisingly, toward Ned, and Elliott felt a flash of guilt at that. She kept some in reserve for Abby, though, who gave back just as good as she got.

"I don't give a flying fuck what you think of me, Francesca," Abby declared, her eyes blazing. "But if you *ever* talk about my son like that again, I will find some way to *end* you."

Francesca's voice rose as she screamed at Abby's retreating back. "I want you and your children out of this house!"

"Oh, we're going!" Abby yelled back, flipping Francesca the bird. "We're *going*!"

Elliott hoped it was before blood was spilled.

Elliott went looking for John and found him hiding away in Henry's study. He let himself in quietly. John was sitting on the couch with a tumbler of whiskey in his hand and the bottle leaning precariously on the cushion beside him.

He gave Elliott a weary look when Elliott entered the room, and picked up the bottle to give him space to sit down.

Elliott sat. "I'm really sorry, John."

John sighed. "I know. I'm sorry too." He cleared his throat. "The family trust won't budge. They were probably never going to, but I had some savings that—" He cut himself off and shook his head. "Well,

Francesca won't let that happen either. Sorry."

Elliott nodded, his throat aching.

"I was supposed to hate it, you know." John swirled his whiskey in his glass. "Whenever I got sent here to visit Dad during school vacations. I was supposed to hate Abby, and I suppose for a long time I did, but she really was the most fun *au pair* I ever had. I was angrier with Dad than I was with her. I kind of wish he'd fought my mother harder for custody."

"I wish he'd been a better father to you," Elliott said, his voice cracking.

"Me too." John took a swig of whiskey. "But that was never your fault."

"I'm sorry about today," Elliott said. "With Ned."

John made a face. "Yeah, that has not gone down well, has it?"

Elliott smiled despite himself. "It really hasn't."

"Robert's the problematic one of the family," John said. "The party boy. Ned's supposed to be the *quiet* one, so this has thrown Francesca for a loop."

Yeah, well. Elliott was surely proof that even the quiet ones could harbor some surprises. Still, he felt guilty for his part in landing Ned in Francesca's sights. That was not a fun place to be. At all.

John sighed again, and held Elliott's gaze. "I know you're not a gold-digger, Elliott. I know Abby isn't either. But the family's always had this carefully constructed narrative, you know?"

"I know."

John took a sip of whiskey. "Ugh. This stuff is awful. Is there really nothing better in the house? I looked in the bureau and all I found was some weed."

"That's Dad's stash."

John blinked slowly. "I'm going to pretend it was to help him get through the chemo."

"Of course it was," Elliott deadpanned, and John snorted out what sounded like a reluctant laugh. "One hundred percent medicinal."

John poured himself another whiskey and offered the open bottle to Elliott. "Where will you end up, do you think?"

"California, I guess. Mom's got a cousin there, in Barton Lake."

"Oh, of course." John nodded. "That's where Abby's from, right?

We used to spend our summers there, right up until Mom and Dad got the divorce. It was one of those towns that was all the rage for like a season or two when people were looking for the next Hamptons or something, then it dropped off the radar again."

"People were looking for the next Hamptons in California?"

John shrugged. "I think it has hot springs or something? It was a big resort town back in the twenties or thirties, and someone tried to revive it, but it didn't take. It is right up near Oregon though. So, you know, not *California* California." He swallowed a mouthful of whiskey. "It was nice, from what I remember."

"I hope so."

"Have you . . ." John faltered for a moment. "Have you got anywhere to stay?"

Elliott wondered what John would say if they didn't, and got an almost vicious thrill out of imagining lying about it. He didn't though, in the end. He couldn't. John was the one member of the Family he could actually stand to be in the same room with. He didn't want to sour their already fragile relationship just to score a few cheap points in this moment.

He remembered the way Henry had held their hands. *My boys. My sons.* John was the only brother he had.

He swallowed. "Mom's cousin has an apartment we can use."

"That's good." John sounded relieved.

"I've made a list of paintings," Elliott said. "Odette from the gallery is sending someone to come get them next week, and there are a few that have sold already they're going to transport for us. Dad left them to Mom and to us, John. I've labeled them, so you know which ones you can't just throw out."

"I wouldn't."

Elliott supposed that was the truth. But Francesca might, or someone else in the Family, out of sheer spite.

Elliott handed him back the bottle of whiskey. "I should go pack, I guess. I'm assuming that Francesca has doubled down on kicking us out by now, and Mom will need some help."

"I'm sorry, Elliott."

"It's okay." Elliott smiled. "We should probably be out of here by the time Uncle Montgomery discovers the spiders anyway, right?"

John started to nod, and then jolted. "Discovers the *what*?" He stared at Elliott for a moment, eyes wide, and then abruptly sank back into his seat and waved the bottle of whiskey at him. "Greta?"

"Who else?"

"Well, couldn't happen to a nicer guy, I suppose." John wedged the bottle under his arm and held his hand out. "Good luck, Elliott."

Elliott took his hand and pulled him into an embrace. "Take care, John."

It was the closest either of them would ever come, he figured, to an *I love you*.

***

Elliott waited until everyone else was at dinner to return to his room and pack. He didn't have a lot of stuff, not really. Or at least he didn't have a lot of stuff he felt obligated to take with him. There were probably boxes of old toys and school reports and the entire detritus of his youth either shoved in the back of his closet or up in the attic somewhere, but this would be a clean break, right? Minimalist living, unburdened by possessions. This would be good for the soul.

It didn't *feel* good for the soul, but it was either convince himself this was a positive step or punch a few holes in the walls. And Elliott would prefer not drive all the way to California with busted knuckles.

Clothes, a few books, and some knickknacks and trinkets he'd picked up over the years. A stuffed duffel bag and a box. It was less than most kids took to college. Except it was also a hell of a lot more than many people had, so Elliott needed to remember that and excuse himself from the pity party he was throwing in his own head.

California.

A fresh start.

No more Family drama.

He slung his duffel bag over his shoulder and hefted the box into his arms.

He ran into Ned on his way downstairs.

"Hi," Ned said, flushing.

"Hi," Elliott echoed softly.

"I'm really sorry," Ned said, dragging a hand through his hair. "I shouldn't have—" He broke off with something that sounded too bitter, to full of self-recrimination to be a laugh. "What a mess!"

Elliott shrugged and tried to force a smile. "Our family's always been a mess. You just came along at an exciting time."

"I tried telling Francesca that it . . . that it wasn't a *thing*." Ned worried at his lower lip with his teeth. "She, um, wasn't in the mood to listen."

"If it wasn't this, it would have been something else," Elliott said. He and Abby and the girls had been on borrowed time since the funeral, and they'd all known it.

Ned's forehead wrinkled, and he tilted his head as he looked at Elliott. "Don't you ever get angry?"

Elliott's stomach clenched. He shifted the weight of the box in his arms. "What would be the point of getting angry?"

"That's not an answer, Elliott," Ned said softly, and reached out to touch him.

"I've got stuff to do." Elliott stepped around him. "It was . . ." He shrugged again. "It was fun, I guess."

Fun, he thought as he continued on his way. Not a thing.

He could feel Ned's worried gaze on him all the way down the stairs.

Not a thing at all.

***

At ten minutes to midnight, with the Naked Blue Lady wrapped in several protective layers of plastic and canvas and strapped securely to the roof rack of Abby's twelve-year-old Subaru Impreza wagon, Elliott and his mother and his sisters set off for California.

CHAPTER 5

Barton Lake was a small town less than seventy miles from the Oregon border. Mount Shasta dominated the horizon. It was beautiful, probably, but Elliott was too damned exhausted to appreciate it. It had been drizzling for the last hour of the trip, the windshield wipers were only doing their job half as well as they should, and Elliott didn't have a field of vision as much as a narrow arc. And running up the ass of a car in front of them would pretty much be the last thing they needed.

They'd taken it slow, stopping for plenty of breaks, and after three and a half days, Elliott never wanted to get in a car again. He and Abby and Marianne had shared the driving, but Elliott was still bone tired and aching, and sick of gas station food and shitty motel room beds.

After the highway, it felt like they were crawling as they drove into Barton Lake. Main Street was only a few blocks long. The buildings were almost all Art Deco, the uniform facades of low-reliefs with richly embellished chevrons and ziggurats only broken once or twice by a less exuberant modern design. It really was picturesque.

A faded sign pointed out the way to the hot springs.

"There is it!" Abby exclaimed. "That's John's store! Pull over where you can, Elliott."

Elliott found a parking space a few buildings down from the one Abby had pointed out, and climbed out of the car. Marianne and Greta got out of the back, yawning and stretching. Elliott rolled his shoulders and pressed his hands against the ache in his lower back. The cold drizzle was bracing, and Elliott stood in it for a moment before stepping into the shelter of the awnings on the pavement. He dragged his fingers through his hair, and then rubbed his face. The heel of his hand rasped against his jaw. He hadn't bothered to shave since they'd left. God, he hoped the apartment had a decent shower.

He followed Abby and the girls along the sidewalk. There was a spring in Abby's step that he hadn't seen in a while, and when she turned to check he was behind them, she was smiling.

"Here we are!" she exclaimed. "At last!"

The sign hanging from the awning was bright yellow, with the store name painted in cursive: *Lake Springs Crystals and Healing*. The bells on the door jingled as Abby pushed her way inside, and Elliott almost choked on the sweet miasma of incense that escaped from the shop in a warm cloud.

He exchanged a glance with Marianne.

Yep. Their mom was definitely related to the person who owned this store.

Inside the store it was dark, and Elliott's eyes took a moment to adjust. There were shelves and display cases packed tightly into the space and almost overflowing with crystals and dream catchers and intricate figurines of wizards and wolves and dragons. There were incense holders, and hookas, and oil burners, and tea glasses, and tarot cards, and worry dolls, and books, and, on every shelf, crystals of every color and cut imaginable. Pan pipes played softly in the background.

"It's like a hippie exploded," Greta whispered.

Marianne coughed pointedly, but that might have been the incense.

Abby bustled forward toward the counter at the rear of the shop. "John!" she exclaimed.

A large bearded man in a tie-dyed shirt rose from a seat behind the counter and stepped out to meet her, knocking a display of beaded bracelets as he moved and sending them rattling against one other. "Abby!"

They embraced warmly.

"Ah!" John exclaimed, releasing Abby and beaming. "And this must be Marianne, and Margaret—"

"Greta," Greta corrected, stepping forward dubiously for a hug.

"—and Elliott!" John finished.

Elliott found himself briefly enclosed in a fug of patchouli. And weed. Definitely weed.

"How wonderful to meet you all at last," John said. "I'm was so saddened to hear of Henry's passing."

Abby smiled sadly and leaned into John's embrace again. "Thank you for everything, John."

John waved his hand. "No, no. None of that. It's what family does."

Elliott stared at a figurine of a wizard, and it stared back at him.

Not every family.

***

The apartment above the store was small. It had one entrance through the shop, the door hidden behind a beaded curtain behind the counter. The other entrance led down a set of narrow steps into a thin back yard populated with a few stringy weeds and not much else. There was an alleyway behind it, with a pair of dented trash cans by the gate.

The apartment had two smallish bedrooms, a joint living and dining area, a bathroom and toilet, and a small kitchen space. The fixtures looked like they dated back to the seventies, but everything was clean and appeared to be in working order.

Rent free, Elliott reminded himself as he took in the double bed in one bedroom and the bunk beds in the second.

"I call top bunk!" Greta exclaimed.

"I was thinking," Abby said, "that me and you could share the double, Greta."

Greta's face fell.

"I'll take the couch," Elliott said.

Greta was a thirteen-year-old girl. She didn't need to share a bed with her mom.

"Are you sure, Elliott?" Abby asked worriedly.

"I'm sure. It's fine."

The couch was a foldout, and he could keep his clothes and things in one of the bedrooms. It was fine, and it wouldn't be forever. He'd get a job, and get some money coming in, and maybe they could look at getting a bigger place.

Just . . . it wasn't Norland Park. It wasn't *home*. It wasn't the house he'd grown up in, happily heedless of his own privilege until it was ripped away from him. Elliott resented the small voice inside him that

complained this wasn't fair, but at the same time . . . *fuck*, it wasn't
fair. His parents should have been more responsible. They should
have planned for this. Taken out life insurance, or something. But no.
They'd both floated along through life as though nothing could touch
them, and now Elliott was stuck sleeping on a foldout couch in a tiny
little apartment in Barton Lake, California.

Elliott drew his fingers through his hair and forced his resentment
away. He was tired, that was all. He'd been driving for too long, and
he just needed a sleep. Things were always more dire with the added
weight of exhaustion.

"Marianne," Abby said, "you and Greta go and get the bags. If I
remember, there's a grocery store just down the street. I'm going to get
us some bread and cheese and we can have grilled cheese sandwiches
for dinner."

Elliott nodded and dug into the pocket of his jeans for the car
keys. "I'll help with—"

"No." Abby snatched the keys off him. "You've been driving all
day. Have a rest. The girls and I will take care of things."

"Okay," Elliott said. "Thanks, Mom."

Abby stood on tiptoes to kiss him on the forehead.

***

It was getting dark when Elliott woke up to the smell of grilled
cheese and the sound of Abby and Greta jostling in the cramped space
of the kitchen. Elliott blinked out the window that overlooked the
narrow back yard. Gray and drizzling. He uncurled himself from the
couch and stood, stretching until his back cracked. He hadn't bothered
unfold the couch before taking his nap, and he was sore. He'd also
woken with a vague headache. He wondered if the bathroom stuff was
unpacked yet, and if they'd brought any Tylenol.

What time did the stores close in a town as small as Barton Lake?
What time was it *now*?

He dug his phone out of his pocket to check. It wasn't even four
p.m. The clouds and rain were ushering in an early nightfall.

The living room was tiny. Apart from the couch and a shelf for a
television to sit, there was only room for the small table with its four

mismatched chairs. Marianne was already seated, a brightly colored tourist map of Barton Lake spread out on the table. She was eating her grilled cheese, dropping crumbs over all of Barton Lake's landmarks.

"Oh," she said, raising her eyebrows. "We're actually really close to the lake!"

"You could walk it," Abby called from the kitchen. "Not in this weather, though. You'll catch pneumonia."

"That's a myth," Greta informed her. "Pneumonia is caused by a virus or bacteria, not by getting wet."

"Yes, we know," Marianne shot back before Abby could answer.

Greta appeared, glowering, in the doorway. "Then why do people say it, doofus?"

Marianne rolled her eyes. "Why do you call everyone a doofus?"

"Because Mom says I'm not allowed to call everyone a dickweed." Greta stuck her tongue out. "*Doofus.*"

Elliott sat down at the table.

Marianne raised her eyebrows. "We can have her enrolled in school by the end of the week, right?"

Elliott snorted.

Abby swept out of the kitchen and set a plate down on top of the map. She kissed Elliott on the top of the head. "That's yours."

"Hey!" Greta exclaimed, indignant. "Mom! I was waiting for mine!"

"Your brother did most of the driving today. He gets his grilled cheese before you. That's how it works." Abby returned to the kitchen.

"In what? Grilled cheese law?" Greta asked.

"Yes!" Marianne called. "And if you don't like it you can get yourself a grilled cheese lawyer."

Elliott bit into his grilled cheese and studied the map. It was upside down for him, but there wasn't a lot to it. It seemed to be mostly the main street with a few landmarks marked with numbers that corresponded to the cartoonish key that ran down the side of the map. It also showed the lake itself, which appeared to be about a mile away on what was optimistically called the Barton Lake Tourist Route. The Tourist Route ran out at the edge of the map, where the lake was, but a big red arrow and some awful Comic Sans pointed the way to the hot springs and something called the Crystal Caves. Elliott couldn't help imagining the caves like the inside of John's shop: full of incense and wizards. He pushed the image away.

"There is a school here, right?" he asked. "I mean, we definitely need to look into that."

Marianne hummed and shrugged. "Probably."

Elliott needed to draw up a list, because nothing would get done if he waited for Abby and Marianne to get around to it. His dad had laughed at him once, telling him he was making a rod for his own back. It didn't have the impact it should have, though, since at the time they'd been eating dinner by candlelight because his parents had forgotten to pay the power bill. Twice. Elliott's childhood had been a sort of low-level chaos like that. Picking up the phone, he'd never known what it might be about. An unpaid bill, a forgotten appointment, a teacher, or some stoner guy they'd met on holiday in Tibet four years ago letting them know he'd just gotten off the bus in Provincetown and could someone come and pick him up? And none of it *mattered*, since they had enough money to make sure it didn't matter, but still, couldn't anyone ever write a fucking reminder?

It mattered now, though.

Elliott was damn sure it mattered now.

"Don't you ever get angry?" It was Ned Ferrars' voice in his head.

Elliott ate the rest of his grilled cheese and left the table to make room for Greta and Abby. He pushed open the door and went outside, sitting on the small landing at the top of the stairs.

It was cold and still drizzling. Down in the narrow yard, a few small birds hopped about, ruffling their wet feathers and picking through the scant grass for insects or seeds or whatever it was they were chasing.

For all that he had sometimes envied his parents—and Marianne—their reckless, heedless, joyful way of living, that's not who Elliott was. He'd tried, but he just wasn't the type of person who could blow off a few bills and laugh when the power was cut off, or the gas was, and declare it an adventure. It annoyed him because it so unnecessary. It was such a simple thing to avoid having happen. You paid your bills when they came in. You wrote your appointments in a calendar. You packed umbrellas just in case.

"It's just a bit of rain, Elliott!"

Cold drizzle slid down the back of his neck into his shirt.

Just a bit of rain, and here he was sitting in it. Okay, so maybe he was a *little* like his parents. That whole thing with Ned, for example. Francesca would have thrown them out anyway, so there was no point blaming himself for that. And it had been fun, in a crazy sort of way, to just give in to the moment like he had. To do something wild and unexpected and *hot*.

Elliott smiled to himself as he thought of Ned, and watched the little birds hopping around in the rain.

***

Elliott's nap caught up with him in the middle of the night, when he awoke and was unable to get back to sleep. The pattern of light on the ceiling was unfamiliar to him, and he stared at it for a while. The rain had picked up while he'd slept, and was now a steady beat on the roof. It was cool, and Elliott debated whether or not it was worth getting up to dig around in the dark for a blanket. Probably not. He didn't want to wake anyone.

He heard the muffled sounds of Abby snoring from her room. The girls' room was quiet.

Elliott thought of Norland Park. He wondered if he would miss it for the rest of his life. Not just the more than generous dimensions of the house, but the fact that everything Elliott was had been discovered in the sanctuary between its walls. It was more than a house. It was family, and it was happiness, and it was home. Would this tiny apartment ever feel as warm to him? It was hard to imagine it could.

Every milestone in Elliott's life had happened at Norland Park.

Birthdays, Christmases, and rites of passage like getting ready for his first school dance. Then, a few years after that, getting ready for his first school dance with a *guy*. Elliott had first been kissed in the gardens of Norland Park, when he and Sean were shooting hoops behind the old carriage house. He'd lost his virginity the following week when Sean had come for a sleepover. Two awkward, fumbling, sixteen-year-old boys. It'd been more or less a disaster.

Elliott's thoughts drifted to Ned.

Not a disaster. Well, the entire surrounding shit fight had been a disaster, but the actual part where they'd gotten each other off pressed up against Elliott's awful painting? Elliott smiled at the memory. A mess, but not a disaster.

He shifted against the thin mattress of the fold-out couch. The springs wheezed a little, but didn't squeak too loudly. Still . . . he could hear Abby snoring through a closed door. He wasn't going to . . .

He reached down and cupped himself through his pajama pants, and his dick twitched with a sleepy sort of interest.

No.

He didn't even know where his lube was packed.

He rolled onto his back and put his hands behind his head.

He missed his dad, but that was like a low-level buzzing in the back of his consciousness, and had been since Henry died. It was the sort of thing that Elliott didn't believe would ever really heal. It was the sort of thing that he would learn to live with, because that's what people did. It was just . . . Elliott wanted to skip the part where he figured out how to deal, and just get to the end where he knew. He wanted to skip this part, where he was sleeping on a fold out couch in a tiny two-bedroom apartment on the other side of the country. He wanted to skip to the part where his memories of his dad made him smile, not hurt.

Grief was exhausting.

There was a lot of guilt mixed up in there too. A part of Elliott had been glad when Henry died. And he told himself it was because Henry wasn't in pain anymore, but wasn't it also that Elliott didn't have to deal with it anymore? With the chemo, and the hospital, and the sheer fucking agony of waiting for the inevitable. It was done now, it was over, and they could move on.

Selfish.

Was it like this for everyone?

Time, Ned had said, and that seemed like the sort of thing everyone said, but coming out of Ned's mouth it hadn't sounded like a platitude. It had sounded like he cared. That might have been nice to explore. A thing with someone who cared.

Elliott didn't feel cheated or anything for having missed out on the college experience, but it had been socially isolating being at home for the last three years while Henry got sicker and sicker and his needs became the first and the last thing Elliott thought about every day. So maybe it wasn't just relief he'd felt when Henry died. Maybe there was some panic there as well, just a little, just a tiny voice in the back of his head wondering what he was supposed to do now. He'd fallen very gratefully into the role of peacekeeper with the Family—right up until the Ned incident—but now what? Once he got Marianne into college and Greta into school and Abby into a place where she could function again, what about him? Who was he when all that was done? Would he even recognize himself anymore?

He wanted . . . he didn't know what he wanted. He wanted a long term future, but the idea of what that would look like was vague and nebulous and shrank into nothing when he weighed it up against what he needed to get done in the short term. He wanted to be happy?

Jesus.

Kill the fucking question mark.

He wanted to be happy.

Except Elliott wasn't sure what that looked like either.

He watched the pattern of lights on the ceiling.

It didn't matter yet if he didn't know any of the answers. He knew what he had to do in the short term, and that was enough. The rest, he'd figure out along the way. It was a process.

Time, Ned had said, and Elliott figured that was the answer to most questions in life after all.

He closed his eyes and drifted back to sleep.

CHAPTER 6

Their first full day in Barton Lake—a Wednesday—dawned bright, with only a few clouds smudged across the sky. Elliott woke before his mother and sisters, thanks to the sunlight streaming directly through the living area windows and hitting him in the face. Curtains. They needed curtains. He took the opportunity to grab the first shower in the small bathroom. He'd claimed the narrow windowsill as space for his toiletries, seeing as Abby and the girls had already managed to stuff the small vanity cabinet full, and also covered the entire surface around the sink.

Although small, the bathroom was light and airy, and the hot water soothed away all the stiffness remaining in Elliott's back from the long drive. Elliott shaved under the shower, and then toweled himself dry and dressed in jeans and a long-sleeved t-shirt. He padded barefoot back outside, only to find Greta awake, a blanket wrapped around her shoulders, glaring at him from underneath a bird's nest of tangled hair.

"Elliott, I really need to *pee*!" She barged past him into the bathroom.

"Good morning, Greta," he murmured as he made his way to the kitchen.

A few minutes later he heard the toilet flushing, and Greta shuffled into the kitchen where he was making breakfast. She shuffled up and hip-checked him. "Good morning." She wrinkled her nose. "Are we have grilled cheese again?"

"It's literally all we have. We're going to have to get groceries today."

Greta nodded and covered a yawn with her hand.

Abby surfaced while Elliott and Greta were eating. "I got a text from John this morning. He wants to know if one of us will mind the shop with him today."

"I will!" Greta declared.

"No," Abby said. "You and I are going to enroll you in school. I thought Elliott or Marianne could do it."

The door to Marianne and Greta's room was still closed.

"I'll do it," Elliott said. "What time?"

"Ten."

Of course a shop like that didn't open early. Elliott was sort of surprised it actually had enough business to sustain itself. Who put healing crystals and incense on their weekly shopping list? Okay, so people like Abby were totally into all that stuff, but regular people? Nobody else needed a constant supply of sandalwood dhoop cones and wizard figurines, surely.

"Can you and Greta get some groceries today?" Elliott asked.

"Sure," Abby said. "I'll write a list. Do you want anything in particular?"

Elliott shook his head, and rose from his seat so Abby could take his place at the little table. "Oh. Maybe some lemongrass tea?"

Abby threw him a smile. "As if I'd forget to get my baby his favorite tea!"

"I thought I was your baby," Greta groused.

"You are all my babies," Abby said.

"I'm your favorite though, right?" Greta asked, wide-eyed and innocent.

"You're all my favorites," Abby said airily.

Greta rolled her eyes, and Elliott hid a smile as he sat down on the couch. Greta was always trying to trick their parents into declaring her the favorite. It had never worked with their dad, and it was never going to work with Abby either. She was wise to Greta's tricks.

Elliott scrolled through the news on his phone, and wondered if any of the wifi networks showing belonged to the shop. There was one called Crystalz, which sounded like it had potential, but also sounded like it might belong to a seedy strip club or something. It was the fault of the z, probably. The network was password protected, so Elliott made a mental note to ask John about it later. He'd rather not blow through all his data if he could be using John's wifi.

After breakfast, Abby and Greta dressed and headed off to enroll Greta at the local school. Greta looked particularly thunderous and uncooperative, which meant she was more nervous than she wanted to let on.

"Give 'em hell, Greta," Elliott said. "But not *too* much hell."

That earned him what looked to be an unwilling smile before Abby ushered her out the back door and down the stairs.

Elliott set about unpacking his scant boxes. He moved his clothes into Abby's room and took over half the closet. Not ideal, but it'd work for a while. The Naked Blue Lady was leaning up on the wall behind the bed. Elliott considered himself long ago inured to her, but she looked even bigger and more confronting resting on the floor. World's Most Disturbing Headboard. They could charge people money to tangle up in blankets and roll around on Abby's bed until they were free, and call it a rebirthing experience. The crystals and wizards crowd would probably go for it.

The squeal of the pipes in the bathroom alerted him to the fact that Marianne was up. Elliott went back out into the living area and tried his best to fit the rest of his stuff on the small set of shelves under the window. What wouldn't fit on the shelves stayed in the box beside them.

It was workable, but Elliott really needed to look into getting an actual paying job—actual health insurance would be nice too—and then moving everyone into a bigger place.

"Oh, wow," Marianne said, trailing out of the bathroom and into the kitchen wearing only a towel. "Do we seriously only have grilled cheese for breakfast?"

"Mom's getting groceries today."

"Ugh." She stood and dripped on the floor for a moment longer. "I think I saw a coffee shop yesterday. I'm going to buy a bagel."

"Make sure you do it before ten," Elliott told her.

"Why?"

"We're minding the store today, apparently."

"Ugh," Marianne said again, and finally headed off into her bedroom to get dressed.

***

"And this," John announced as he concluded the tour of the crowded little shop, "is the cash register! She's a little bit temperamental, so you need to smack her on the side to get the drawer to open. You'll soon get the hang of it!" He beamed at a dubious Elliott and Marianne. "Let me show you how to run a charge card." And then, barely thirty minutes later: "Right, then! You seem to have a handle on things. I'm taking the day off!"

And that was it.

The bells above the shop door jangled as John made his escape into the cold fresh air outside, and then Elliott and Marianna were alone, and in charge.

Elliott eyed a smoking stick of incense, and then picked the little brass stand up and shifted it further down the counter.

"Ooh!" Marianne exclaimed, ducking out from behind the counter to inspect the rack of books nearest them. "Look, Elliott! *A Beginner's Guide to Tantric Sex.*" She plucked the book off the rack and turned it over to check the back. "It's thirty dollars!"

"Who would—"

"Seems like a solid investment," Marianne said with a grin. "It'd pay for itself in mind-blowing orgasms, right?"

Elliott sighed.

"Although . . ." Marianne flicked through the book. "Who'd want to have sex for like twenty hours at a time?"

"Twenty?" Elliott asked. "*Hours?*"

"Wouldn't you get hungry?" Marianne paused on a page. "Do you think chafing would be an issue? It can't be penetration that whole time, right?"

"Sometimes I wish I'd been born on the repressed WASP side of the family," Elliott told her.

"Liar." Marianne put the book down again and began to browse the shelves. "So do you think we'll get any actual customers, or—" She straightened up as the bells on the door jangled and an older couple stepped inside. "Good morning!"

Elliott sat on the stool behind the counter and watched as Marianne spoke with the customers. She was always good with new people. Better than Elliott, at any rate. Just like their parents: every stranger was a new best friend. She chattered away happily with the older couple—tourists—and directed them toward the shelf of figurines carved by local artists from crystal sourced from the caves up past the springs. She sounded like she'd lived in Barton Lake her whole life. Not bad for someone who'd only read the same tourist map these people had. Her friendliness encouraged them to spend over eighty dollars on little crystal figurines of a deer, a wolf, and a bird.

"This is fun," Marianne announced a while later as she trailed a feather duster along one of the shelves. "Remember when we were little and we had that toy grocery store with the plastic counter and register and everything?"

Elliott smiled. "I remember Mom threw the register away and said we should give all our groceries away for free because capitalism was evil."

Marianne laughed. "Right!"

Elliott's smile faded. He dug around in a small basket of worry stones beside the register, and found one that was marked down to a dollar. There was a crack in the sloping indentation on its surface. Elliott held the stone and rubbed his thumb over it, mapping the dimensions of the crack. It was almost soothing in a way. Cracked. Imperfect. Still solid. Elliott was almost tempted to pay a dollar for the thing. He slipped it back into the basket instead.

He wondered how Abby and Greta were going at the school.

"Have you thought about college?" he asked.

Marianne looked up from her dusting. "Well it's not like we've got the money for it, is it?"

"No." Elliott rolled his shoulders. "There are community colleges, though. With payment plans. And there are loans and scholarships."

"I probably won't go."

"You should."

"Well, so should you," Marianne said. She raised her eyebrows. "You gave up college to help look after Dad, so why shouldn't I do the same to help look after Mom?"

"Because I'm already doing it, Mar." Elliott rearranged some brochures on the counter: *Visit the Hot Springs and the Crystal Caves! At Beautiful Barton Lake!* The same Comic Sans and rainbow lettering as the tourist map. The Barton Lake Tourism Board needed to lift their game.

Marianne wrinkled her nose. "College will still be there in a year. I mean, Dad just *died*, Elliott." She held his gaze, a strange longing in her face, as though she was willing him to understand something she couldn't quite articulate.

Elliott thought he did.

Life was short. Life was fragile. Their dad's death had Elliott wanting to hunker down, to find shelter, to somehow protect himself from being hurt again. It made him want to take the people he still had and hold them as closely as he could. Grief made Elliott defensive, afraid of making a misstep. It made Marianne braver, unanchored and reckless with it, and greedy to live as much as she could while she could. It made her want to spread her wings and fly.

Elliott had always envied Marianne her courage, while at the same time it worried him how much faith she put in the world, in people, in the universe making sure things worked out in the end.

"I know," Elliott said softly.

"I'm not saying I won't go to college," Marianne said, the corner of her mouth lifting. "Just that I won't *now*."

Elliott nodded. "Okay."

"Okay?" she echoed, like she didn't believe he'd give in so easily.

"It's your decision."

The quirk of Marianne's mouth became an actual smile. "It is," she agreed, and then picked up a figurine of a wizard. She waggled it in Elliott's direction and dropped her voice to a gruff rumble: "I agree with Marianne."

"Nobody asked you," Elliott told it.

"Ignore my brother," Marianne stage-whispered to the wizard as she set it back on the shelf with its fellows. "He doesn't even believe in magic."

***

The bells on the shop door jangled. Elliott straightened up from where he was reorganizing the incense in the pigeonholes beside the counter, but Marianne breezed out from behind the bead curtain and beat him to the customer.

"Hi," she said brightly. "Can I help you?"

The woman stopped, frowned down at the piece of paper she was holding, and then lifted her gaze again. "I'm looking for John? John Middleton?"

"John's not here at the moment." Marianne smiled. "Were you looking for anything in particular?"

The woman looked around the store dubiously. "I called last week. John was putting a DVD aside for me."

"Hmm," Marianne said. "Elliott, is there anything behind the counter?"

Elliott bent down to check. He found a cardboard box with *"On Hold – don't sell!!!!"* scrawled on the side in sharpie. He pulled it out and set it on the counter. There were a few DVDs in there, along with a tin of ginger and honey tisane, a book about astral projection, a frog magnet, and a pack of tarot cards. All the items had sticky notes attached to them. Elliott flipped through the DVDs. "It might be one of these. Can I have your name?"

"Brandon," the woman said. She was in her late thirties, maybe her early forties. She had sandy-colored hair cut short on the sides and left longer on top. She was dressed in khakis and a button-up shirt ironed so precisely that the darts looked as sharp as blades. She moved closer toward the counter, her gait a little uneven and her mouth tightening. "Deanna Brandon."

Elliott flipped through the DVDs again. There was one labeled *Lt. Col. Brandon*. The military rank certainly seemed like a good fit for the woman standing in front of the counter. The title of the DVD—*Finding your Center: Viniyoga and Meditation Techniques for Beginners*—did not.

"Um, is this it?" Elliott asked, holding it up so she could see the cover.

Colonel Brandon's mouth thinned. Her brows drew together, and a hint of color rose in her cheeks. "I'm supposed to learn how to *relax*."

She said the word like it was an obscenity.

"Viniyoga's very good," Marianne offered with a bright smile. "It's not as physically intense as something like vinyasa or ashtanga, and it's a great way to really learn how to *move*, you know?"

Colonel Brandon just stared at her. Clearly she did not know.

"I'm supposed to relax," she said again, awkwardly.

Marianna's smile didn't even falter. "Well, in that case, yoga is fine, but you know what's really great?"

Elliott really hoped she didn't produce the book on tantric sex.

"What?" Colonel Brandon asked gruffly.

"Weed," Marianne said.

Colonel Brandon blinked at her slowly. "That . . . that's not something I'm going to do."

"Okay," Elliott said, setting the DVD case down on the counter. "That's, um, $19.99."

Colonel Brandon cast a wary look in Marianne's direction, then tugged her wallet out of the pocket of her khakis. She pulled a perfectly crisp twenty dollar bill out of it and slid it over the counter.

Elliott rang up her purchase, dropped the penny change she didn't want in the donation tin for Oxfam, and shoved the DVD and the receipt in a paper bag.

"Have a great day!" Marianne called to Colonel Brandon's back as she retreated out onto the street again.

The bells jangled aggressively as the door swung shut.

"Really?" Elliott asked.

"What?"

"Can you maybe not tell the customers to get high? It's not very professional."

Marianne snorted and gestured around at the store. "Oh, please. As if the customers don't expect us to be total potheads."

Elliott reached for the cracked worry stone. "The only reason we've got a place to live is because we're working in the store, remember? Don't give John a reason to fire us."

"You worry too much, Elliott," Marianne said airily.

Probably. But only because nobody else worried at all.

Elliott ran his thumb over and over the crack in the stone.

**

They ate better that night than they had in days. With the specter of greasy diner and gas station food behind them, Abby whipped up a tofu stir fry with a ginger and honey sauce. It was packed with spinach and snow peas, and Elliott never wanted to look at another grilled cheese in his life.

They somehow all crowded around the tiny table as they ate. Marianne filled Abby and Greta in on their adventures in the store, and Abby and Greta filled Marianne and Elliott in on their adventures in getting Greta enrolled in the local junior high.

"It looks like it was built when the rest of the town was," Greta supplied, waving her fork dangerously close to Elliott's field of vision. "It's probably six hundred percent asbestos, and when I die you can sue the school district for a gazillion dollars."

"At least you won't have died in vain," Marianne said approvingly.

"They're putting me in honors classes," Greta said, and wrinkled her nose.

Abby leaned over and knocked her gently with her shoulder. "You'll do great in honors classes, baby."

Greta glowered.

"I'm going to talk to John tomorrow about how often he needs us to work in the store," Elliott said. "Mom, maybe you and Marianne can take most of the hours there, and I'll look for something that pays?"

Abby raised her eyebrows. "Or maybe you can take a week or two and do nothing, Elliott. Have you thought of that?"

Marianne and Greta were watching him curiously, and Elliott suddenly realized what this was: an ambush. They'd clearly been discussing him behind his back, and painting him as some work-obsessed penny-pincher.

"What?" he asked, setting his fork down.

"I don't want you working too hard," Abby said firmly.

"No, Mom, Jesus." He snorted. "I'm talking about trying to do the bare minimum, okay? It's not like I'm going to turn into some sort of evil capitalist overlord. It's not like I belong on that side of the Family."

"Elliott, sweetheart." Abby reached out and put her hand over his. "Nobody thinks that."

Elliott tugged his hand free, a hot burst of an emotion he didn't want to name rising up inside him.

"Don't you ever get angry?"

"Elliott," Abby said softly.

Elliott drew a breath.

Nobody thinks that, Abby had said. Nobody thought that Elliott belonged with *those* Dashwoods. The cold-blooded Dashwoods.

Maybe *he* did.

Maybe a part of Elliott—a bigger part of him than he wanted to admit—would have sold his soul right now for a fraction of *those* Dashwoods' financial security.

"It's fine, Mom," he said. He forced a smile and picked up his fork to continue his meal.

CHAPTER 7

On Friday night, John invited the Dashwoods to dinner to properly welcome them to Barton Lake and, as he said, back into the family. For once, that word—absent of that capital F and all its associated connotations that flashed neon-bright in Elliott's mind—sounded genuinely warm.

"Do you still live in that little place on Martin Street?" Abby asked.

"Oh, no," John told her with a laugh. "We're at the Boathouse now! Do you remember the Boathouse?"

"I think so," Abby said, but she had to consult their little tourist map before driving them out there in the evening.

The Boathouse was on Pier Lane, a wide winding street that hugged the first curve of Barton Lake. There were no other houses on the street that Elliott could see. Most of Pier Lane appeared to be public land, with picnic tables and the occasional playground equipment arrayed along the lakeside. The sun was going down as they arrived at the house, and the lake was lit up with pink and gold fire. It was beautiful.

The house was large. It was built in the same deco style as much of the main street. It was stunning.

"This is it," John said proudly as he ushered the Dashwoods inside. "The Boathouse. It was built in the thirties for the people who came to use the lake. There were changing rooms here, and an open air cinema that showed movies at night. There was a kiosk that sold soda and cotton candy, and you could even rent a rowboat for the day!" They passed underneath a decorative lintel. "It was in a hell of a state when Paula and I bought it. We practically had to rebuild it from scratch."

"Oh, it was falling apart the last time I saw it!" Abby exclaimed, distracted by the pressed tin panels in the ceiling. "It's amazing!"

"It's taken the past twenty years to get it into shape," John said. "The county wanted to knock it down. And now look at it! When the girls all head off to college, we're thinking of opening it as a B&B."

Elliott took in his fill of the interior. It was beautifully restored. John might have been an old hippie on the outside, but clearly he was channeling the ghost of Jay Gatsby underneath his faded t-shirts, beaded bracelets, and Birkenstocks.

Then again, maybe Paula Middleton had been in charge of the restoration.

Paula was a bottle blonde in her mid-fifties. She wore her hair in a sleek, neat bob, and dressed like a realtor in a grey skirt suit and a salmon blouse. She couldn't have looked like a more unlikely match for John if she'd tried.

"It's so wonderful to meet you all," she effused, her smile bright. "Welcome! Elliott, and you must be Marianne? And Greta! Abby, goodness, has it really been twenty years? You haven't changed a bit! Come out to the deck and meet the girls!" Her heels tapped on the floor as she led them through. "Rose and Jasmine are away at college, but Poppy and Violet are both still at home."

Elliott couldn't help catch Greta's gaze as she gave a gasp of something between delight and horror.

"Elliott!" she whispered, her eyes wide. "They have *literal* flower children!"

Elliott hung back a little as they arrived at the back deck. Poppy and Violet were blonde like their mother. Poppy wore her hair pulled back tightly. Violet's hair was loose, spilling in haphazard twists. Age wise, they slotted in between Marianne and Greta. Poppy was in her senior year in high school. Violet was a junior. They seemed polite, perhaps even a little standoffish in comparison to their exuberant father, but—Elliott shrugged inwardly—teenagers. Not that he was that much older, but the past few years . . . Elliott's adolescence felt as distant and strange as a foreign country.

"What would you like to drink, Elliott?" Paula said, taking him by the elbow and guiding him toward the large table in the center of the deck. In the dying light it was illuminated by candles in colored glass holders. A kaleidoscope of light fragments danced on the tabletop.

"How about a glass of wine? Red or white? Hmmm. White, I think."

Before Elliott could even confirm, a long-stemmed wine glass was pressed into his hand.

"You look so much like your father," Paula said. Her small smile was almost apologetic. "We were so sorry to hear of his loss."

"Thank you." Elliott sipped his wine.

He watched as John drew Abby over toward the railing of the deck. It overlooked the lake, and the view was beautiful. The sunset was fading into darkness now, and across the wide expanse of water, Elliott could see the faint glimmer of lights. John pointed the lights out to Abby, and she leaned out over the railing as though she were trying to immerse herself in them.

Chair legs dragged on the deck as the girls took up a position at the other end of the table.

Paula followed Elliott's gaze across the lake. "Those are the big houses. Summer places mostly, nowadays, but there are a few year-round occupants. Mrs. Smith. Colonel Brandon. The Bells. The Challenors. Your father and his first wife had a place right on the lakeshore. It was sold, oh, about fifteen years ago now, I think it was."

Too many bad memories? Or just wiping the scandal of Abby and Henry clean? Probably the second one. Paula might have thought the house was owned by Henry, but it wouldn't have been. Everything the Dashwoods owned was managed by the family trust. And what the family trust giveth, the family trust sure as shit taketh away again.

"It's a shame," Paula said with a sigh, and for a moment Elliott thought she was talking about his dad. Then she sipped her wine and sighed again. "There was something so vibrant about this place back when all the big names were here. We would love to get some of those families back. It'd really drive up property values for everyone else, and make Barton Lake a prestige travel destination again."

For a moment Elliott was so still he imagined he could hear the shallow waves on the lake lapping against the shore. The sharp bob, the suit, the talk of property values . . .

Then Paula shook her head, and her expression softened. "I'm sorry. I promised John I wouldn't talk about work. I'm on the Tourism Board, you know."

For a moment Elliott might have mistaken Paula Middleton for someone from his father's side of the Family, but the Barton Lakes Tourism Board and their overuse of clip art and comic sans? Paula was no circling shark.

When she reached out to refill her wine glass, her sleeve rode up, and he caught a glimpse of an intricately detailed hamsa tattoo on her inner wrist. The suit was a lie. Elliott had no doubt her weekend wardrobe was full of cheesecloth.

"John!" Paula called out, and both John and Abby turned from the railing. "I was just saying, isn't Elliott the spitting image of Henry?"

Elliott's heart skipped a beat, but he looked at Abby to find she was smiling.

She stepped toward him, mouth quirked. "Hmm. When I met him, Henry already had gray hairs. He was still a young man, and he already had gray hairs and frown lines." She ruffled her fingers through Elliott's hair. "But he was very handsome, yes. Just like my darling baby boy."

Elliott flushed, and risked a glance at his sisters and the Middleton girls. "Mom!"

"I only do it because I love you," Abby told him, and plucked his wine glass from his grasp long enough to take a sip. Her eyes were bright. "And because it embarrasses you."

Elliott stole his glass back. He was tall enough—or she was short enough—that he could hold it out of her reach. He put his free arm around her shoulders and drew her in for a quick hug.

For a moment they were both distracted by the lights on the far shore of the lake. Elliott didn't have to wonder what his mom was seeing when she looked at them. Who she was seeing. Elliott's heart ached for his father as well.

Abby squeezed him on the forearm, a soft gesture of comfort and reassurance, and then stepped away from him, already laughing in reply to something Marianne had said.

Elliott relaxed, drank his wine, and listened to the conversation flow around him. The candles burned brighter as the night darkened, and their laughter traveled across the lake.

***

Saturday morning dawned bright. Elliott yawned and stretched until the springs in the fold-out couch sang, and decided that after a few too many of Paula's white wines the night before, he needed a coffee to kick start the day. He climbed out of bed and showered quickly, wincing every time the pipes squealed and hoping he wasn't waking everyone up.

When he came back out into the living area, both bedroom doors were still closed, and he couldn't hear any signs of life apart from Abby's snoring.

There was a stack of binders on the small dining table courtesy of Poppy and Violet, for Greta's use at school. They'd taken some of the same classes and had happily handed over their notes. They'd also spent a good deal of last night telling Greta exactly which teachers to avoid riling up. Greta had been unusually willing to listen.

Elliott ran a hand through his hair as he waited for the coffee pot to finish percolating.

They needed to keep an eye on Greta. She liked to pretend she was tough as hell and twice as evil, but underneath her prickly exterior she was a thirteen-year-old girl who'd just lost her dad, her home, and everything she'd ever known. If Elliott was feeling lost still, unanchored, confused by the way the world had so suddenly shifted, then of course Greta was too. And add to all that the stress of starting at a new school, having to make new friends . . . Elliott didn't envy her that at all.

He drank his coffee while he checked the news headlines on his phone, and then went outside. He didn't need to be at the store for another two hours yet, so he walked through the narrow yard and into to the back alley instead. He stuck his hands in his coat pockets and enjoyed the bite of the cool air.

They alley was narrow, cluttered with dumpsters and cars parked haphazardly in the spaces between the rundown back entrances of the businesses fronting Main Street. Elliott walked down it until he reached an unfenced gap between two properties, and turned down there.

He found himself on Main Street, between a restaurant and a bookstore. They were both still closed, but Elliott killed a few minutes checking out the window of the bookstore. It seemed to be a secondhand place, and the display appeared to be as eclectic as the selection of titles. A stack of old Hardy Boys and Nancy Drews spilled out of a battered old red Radio Flyer wagon. A Lego robot stood atop a tower of pulp science fiction novels from the fifties and sixties. Elliott couldn't quite tell if the aura of nostalgia was intentional or not, or if was ironic. It made him want to come back when the store was open and check out their shelves. Elliott had always liked books. Norland Park had a library, but it hadn't been the fancy sort of library most people assumed. Okay, so there had definitely been shelves with matching sets of leather-bound tomes. But there had also been shelves full of kids' books, and comics, and Boys' Own Adventure books that dated back to God only knew when and had been almost read to death by generations of Dashwoods.

It was strange to think that at some point Uncle Montgomery must have read the same stories Elliott had. Maybe they'd even been bought for him. It was strange to think of Montgomery as a child. It was difficult enough to think of him as a human being, in all honesty.

Elliott turned away from the bookstore, and his gaze was caught by a sign in the window of the restaurant: *Now Hiring.* There was a cell phone number scrawled at the bottom. Elliott entered the number in his contacts list. It was probably too early to call now, but he could do it later. He didn't have any experience working in a restaurant— he didn't have any experience working *anywhere*—but since the sign didn't specify they were after a chef or anything, hopefully it was washing dishes or waiting tables or something he could learn on the job.

He walked slowly down Main Street, wondering if it would ever feel familiar to him. If it would ever feel like home.

Barton Lake was a postcard pretty town, but Elliott would be lying if he said he wanted to be here. There were worse places to be by far, but that wasn't the point, was it? He missed Massachusetts. He missed Norland Park. He missed his dad.

When he finally made his way back to the tiny apartment above the store, Abby was sitting at the table with a mug of coffee held between her hands. She was staring into it with the intensity of a fortuneteller, as though she expected it to offer up all the secrets of the universe.

"How's your head?" Elliott asked.

Abby groaned. "Why did Paula think opening that second bottle was a good idea?"

"You agreed with her," Elliott pointed out.

"Well clearly I shouldn't be trusted."

"Clearly." Elliott sat down opposite her. "I went for a walk on Main Street. There's a restaurant that's hiring. I'm going to call them later."

"Oh, that's great." Abby smiled like he already had the job in the bag.

"They haven't hired me yet, Mom."

"They'd be lucky to have you!"

Elliott rolled his eyes at that, and they sat in silence for a moment. Abby sipped her coffee.

"I was talking with Paula last night and she mentioned there's a whole parcel of land right on the lake shore that the town wants to sell for development," Abby said at last. "But nobody's been biting. Is that the business terminology? Biting?"

Elliott shrugged.

"Well, I mentioned to her that we knew the Ferrars family."

Elliott tensed.

"They're in property development, aren't they?"

"I don't know." Elliott thought of Ned's tentative smile, of their kiss in the greenhouse, of their whatever-the hell-it-was in Henry's study. "We didn't really talk about it."

"Well, they are," Abby said. "So I'm going to pass on their contact details." She raised her eyebrows. "If that's okay with you."

"It's nothing to do with me," Elliott said. He wondered if he sounded too defensive. Stupid. There was nothing to be defensive about. "Mom, I know you and Marianne think that Ned Ferrars and I are having some big romance or whatever, but it wasn't like that. It was just a . . . a *thing*."

Abby regarded him closely for a moment. The corner of her mouth twitched, and then she nodded. "Okay, baby."

"Okay?" Elliott repeated warily.

Abby smiled. "Okay."

Elliott relaxed.

Okay.

***

Trade was surprisingly brisk at Lake Springs Crystals and Healing on a Saturday morning. Customers bought a few DVDs, a bunch of touristy knickknacks, and Elliott actually sold more incense than he burned.

He thought about Ned as he worked. About how he liked the guy, about how it has been . . . not fun, exactly—not when everything was still so crowded with grief and confusion—but *nice*? Or hopeful, maybe, to be reminded that just because his entire world was made out of grief and confusion now, great ugly swathes of it like paint applied too thickly to a canvas, that didn't mean it would last forever. There were glimpses of color behind the stark black and the muddied brown of the present, and Ned had helped him to see them. Elliott would always be grateful for that.

There was no future in it though. He had no idea if he'd even meant anything at all to Ned, and it wasn't as though Elliott was in any way emotionally stable enough at the moment to be even considering something as crazy as a relationship. Even *thinking* the word was ludicrous.

It was what it was. Just a moment in time when their lives intersected briefly. It didn't mean anything. Still, there was an unaccountable thrumming in Elliott's chest when he thought of the possibility of running into Ned again. A warmth, and a nervous tension. A sort of strange, breathless hope that had no place taking root there.

Elliott pushed his thoughts of Ned away, and tried to concentrate on working instead. The only problem with that was there wasn't a whole lot to do in the store. There was a steady procession of customers, so it would have been rude to pull the vacuum cleaner out, but it wasn't busy enough to keep him completely distracted from his thoughts. There were only so many times he could rearrange the DVD rack, after all.

Eight times.

He rearranged it eight times before Marianne appeared just after midday with his lunch.

"I made you some bruschetta to apologize for being late," she told him, setting the plate down on the counter. "I'm later than I intended because I had to go and buy some tomatoes."

Elliott picked up a piece of bruschetta. "Worth it," he said, and bit into it.

Marianne flashed him a smile and bounced forward to greet the next customers who walked into the store. "Hello! Is there anything I can help you with?"

Elliott ate his lunch and flicked through an astrology magazine.

Greta clomped down the interior steps in her thick-soled boots shortly afterward, Abby behind her.

"We're going to get Greta some things she needs for school on Monday," Abby announced. "Then how about we take over here and you and Marianne can have the afternoon off?"

"Marianne's been here for a whole twenty minutes," Elliott deadpanned.

"But I made you lunch!" Marianne called out from the other end of the store, from somewhere between the dream catchers and the tarot cards.

Greta stomped toward the exit. Just before she reached it, the door was pushed open, balls jangling, and a woman stepped inside. It was Lieutenant Colonel Brandon. She looked as uncomfortable as last time, eyeing Greta and Abby suspiciously as they swept past her out into the street.

"Hi!" Marianne's smile was as welcoming as always. "You're back soon. How did the yoga go?"

"It was . . ." Colonel Brandon's brows drew together, and her forehead creased. "Fine. It was fine." She cleared her throat. "I was wondering if you had the next one in the series."

"I have no idea," Marianne said. "I'll have a look."

"The last time I was here . . ." Colonel Brandon cleared her throat again. "I didn't get your name."

"Oh, I'm Marianne." Her smile grew. "Marianne Dashwood. And this is my brother Elliott."

Elliott smiled politely.

"Dashwood?" A faint look of surprise crossed Colonel Brandon's face. "As in the Massachusetts Dashwoods?"

"That's us," Marianne said. "Well, that's *them*. I guess we're the California Dashwoods now, right, Elliott?"

"I guess so," Elliott said.

The California Dashwoods.

It didn't sound so bad.

***

On Saturday afternoon, Elliott walked back to the restaurant on Main Street and spoke to the owner. On Sunday night, he worked a trial shift as a waiter. At the end of the night, he was put on the regular roster.

On Monday, Greta started school and Abby watched the store for John.

On Wednesday, Marianne talked herself into three shifts a week at the cinema, working the concession stand.

On Thursday, Elliott got a text message from an unknown number: *This is Ned Ferrars. I got your number from John. I'm going to be in Barton Lake next month for work, and I was hoping to visit you and your family.*

And suddenly that stupid crawling hope was back, beating in his chest like a second heartbeat.

Elliott had no idea what to do with it at all.

CHAPTER 8

"California Dreamin'" was playing on the radio when Elliott left the restaurant, stinking of garlic and carbonara sauce and with a lousy forty-three dollars in tips after an eight-hour shift. It was almost midnight on a Saturday. It was drizzling again, and cold. Elliott turned his collar up, shoved his hands into his pockets, and started out for home. The night was dark, and Elliott picked his way carefully down the narrow path that led to the alley behind Main Street. There was no lighting back here. A cat slunk across Elliott's path. The rain-slick asphalt shone like oil. It was hard to reconcile the fantasy of the dreamer who wanted to escape to the warmth of California with a place like Barton Lake.

Elliott had seen more sunlight back in Massachusetts.

Toward the end, before Henry had gone into the hospital for the last time, he'd liked to spend time on the lawn of Norland Park with his paints and a canvas on an easel. Elliott's memories of those slow afternoons were warm and sun-dappled. He remembered his father's hands, fingers long and thin and speckled with paint.

"It's a beautiful day, Elliott." A slow smile. "It's a beautiful world."

Elliott didn't think the ache would ever completely go away.

He had always connected a little easier with his father than with his mother. Or Henry had understood his quietness more than Abby, or something. Abby had spent much of Elliott's childhood trying to bring him out of his shell, trying to free some wildness of spirit in him that she was sure he was repressing. Always reminding him he could color outside of the lines, or throw away the Lego instructions. Henry hadn't pushed. He'd understood, more than Abby, that Elliott wasn't wired that way.

Henry had relied on it, in the end.

"You'll look after them, won't you, Elliott? When all this is done?"
"Of course I will, Dad."

Henry had reached out and cupped his cheek with his hand. *"And you'll look after yourself too, won't you?"*

Elliott had nodded, his throat too tight to answer.

"I love you, Elliott." He'd left a smudge of paint on Elliott's cheek when he'd removed his hand.

There hadn't been nearly enough of those long afternoons on the lawn.

The soles of Elliott's shoes crunched against the grit of the asphalt. He turned into the yard behind the store and the apartment, and dug his keys out of his pocket as he climbed the steps.

The light in the living room was on, and the television—loaned by one of John's daughters—was on. Some late night talk show host was delivering his monolog while Elliott turned the key in the lock. He pushed the door open to find Marianne sitting cross-legged on the couch in her pajamas, a bowl of popcorn on her lap.

"How was work?" she asked, patting the couch beside her.

Elliott hung his jacket on the hook by the door and toed his shoes off. He glanced at the table and saw that the paperwork he'd picked up for their mom to apply for Greta's Social Security survivor benefit was still untouched. Just looking at it gave him a headache, but he knew that if he didn't push Abby, it would never get done. He sighed, sitting down on the couch with Marianne and reaching for a handful of popcorn. "It was okay."

"You smell like garlic."

He shrugged.

"I'll go to bed if you're tired," Marianne offered.

"It's okay."

They watched TV in silence for a while.

"You should get out more," Marianne said at last.

"I get out plenty." Elliott rolled his eyes. "I just got home."

"Greta and I are going to the Crystal Caves tomorrow. What are you doing?"

"Working."

Marianne tilted her head and narrowed her eyes, as though Elliott were a particularly interesting specimen of some sort. "And does the inside of a Californian restaurant look any different than a Massachusetts one?"

Elliott rolled his eyes.

"Elliott, we moved all the way across the country, and you haven't even left Main Street!" She waved her hand. "Even the light is different here. The way it filters through the leaves. The way everything here is more *golden*. Have you even noticed? Have you even really been outside? You know, stopped and smelled the flowers?"

"I'm *working*, Mar," he said, keeping his tone even and pushing his sudden burst of irritation down. This wasn't . . . it wasn't a *holiday*. Someone had to earn a wage while Marianne seized the fucking day.

He reached for another handful of popcorn, hoping that was just his tiredness talking. He didn't want to resent Marianne. He didn't want to clip her wings either, not when she was only trying to help. It wasn't fair to think of her as selfish. She wasn't. She was one of the most generous people Elliott knew. She was just . . . she was *Marianne*. Abby had never had to encourage Marianne to color outside the lines.

"Guess what happened to me today?" Marianne asked.

"What?"

"There's a Turkish restaurant over in Whitwell." Marianne caught his look. "It's the next town, Elliott. You'd know these things if you went outside. Anyway, one of their belly dancers quit and they offered me a job!"

"Do you even know how to belly dance?"

"One of the other girls is teaching me." She smiled. "They have dancers in every Friday night, and Jody said last Friday she made over a hundred dollars in tips."

"It's not stripping, is it?"

"No." Marianne looked thoughtful. "That would pay a lot better, actually, wouldn't it?"

"Don't be a stripper, Mar."

"Don't be a prude, Elliott," she shot back. "I'd be an awesome stripper." She shimmied her shoulders and leaned back. "My milkshake brings all the boys to the yard, Elliott."

Elliott raised his eyebrows. "Not this one."

Marianne shrugged. "You're not my target audience."

"Thank God."

"Thank God," Marianne echoed, and they both laughed and settled back to watch some more television.

***

A crunch of tires on dirt, and Elliott startled into wakefulness and pushed himself up off the folded-out couch. It was day, and the apartment was full of light. The gauzy curtain in the window fluttered a little in the breeze.

Elliott heard the dull sound of car doors being shut.

"I'm fine!" Marianne's voice was pitched high with stress. "I'm fine, really!"

Elliott pushed open the back door.

There was some type of sporty silver car pulled into the narrow yard. A Porsche, maybe. And there was Marianne, limping away from it, while some guy—the owner of the Porsche, probably—offered himself as a makeshift crutch.

Greta climbed out of the back seat of the Porsche.

"I'm fine!" Marianne said again, sounding more flustered, and possibly close to tears.

Elliott started down the steps just as the guy replied to Marianne. He spoke too quietly for Elliott to hear what he said, but suddenly he was sweeping Marianne up into a bridal carry—she gave a squawk of surprise—and carrying her up the steps.

"Mar?" Elliott asked.

"Sprained my ankle!" she said with a grimace, an arm looped around the guy's neck. "Met a hot guy!"

The guy in question let out a huff of laughter as he swept her through the doorway and into the apartment. Elliott held the door open for Greta.

"It's been an emotional rollercoaster," Greta deadpanned, stomping in after them.

The guy set Marianne down carefully and looked around for Elliott. "Do you have ice?"

"I'll get it," Greta said.

"What happened, Mar?" Elliott asked.

Marianne hobbled toward the folded-out couch and sank down

with a chorus of wheezing spring. She lifted her leg onto the bed, wincing, and tugged up her jeans. "Ow. Ow ow ow."

Elliott leaned down to inspect her ankle. It was swollen and bruised.

"I offered to take her to the hospital," the guy said, "but she said it wasn't that bad."

"It's fine!" Marianne insisted. "It's only a sprain! And it was enough that you brought me home, really."

Greta reappeared, elbowing between Elliott and the guy. She was holding a bag of frozen peas, which she set down on Marianne's ankle. Marianne winced again.

"I'm Jack," the guy said at last, holding his hand out. "Jack Willoughby."

"Elliott Dashwood," Elliott said, shaking his hand.

Jack looked to be around Elliott's age, maybe a year or two older. He was good-looking. He had dark hair, long enough on top to be tousled by the wind, but the undercut itself neat and fresh. His features were defined, any sharpness in them mitigated by a nose that was more snub than straight, and his broad, easy smile.

"It's good to meet you," Jack said. A worried line creased his forehead as he looked back to Marianne. "Are you sure you don't need to go to the hospital?"

"It's fine," Marianne repeated. She reached out and curled her fingers around his wrist. "I'm fine."

Greta took Elliott's pillow and eased it under Marianne's ankle.

Marianne's mouth tightened, and she huffed out a breath. "The caves are lovely, Elliott. Slippery as hell though!" She smiled at Jack. "I'm lucky Jack was there."

Marianne looked at Jack, and he looked back, and their gazes caught and held. There was a moment between them, laden as a lacuna in an orchestral piece. It was weighted enough for Greta to roll her eyes, and for Elliott to excuse himself and go and fetch some Tylenol from the tiny bathroom.

He stared into the age-spotted mirror above the sink and wondered if he and Ned had ever had a moment like that—what a moment like that even was. Attraction? Chemistry? More than that? A *connection*, or at least the start of one? How was anyone supposed to know? Would Elliott recognize it if it ever happened for him?

Or maybe it had, and he'd let it pass unnoticed.

He turned the Tylenol over in his hand, and thought of Ned. He replayed their kiss in the greenhouse, and their moment of craziness in Henry's study. Had there been more there? Did it matter if there wasn't?

Did Ned think of him too?

For some reason, the possibility made his heart skip a beat.

Stupid.

Stupid and pointless.

Elliott stared at his reflection a moment longer before he turned away and took the Tylenol to Marianne.

Jack was spending the summer with his aunt, Sophia Smith, who had a house on Allenham Road, which overlooked the northern side of the lake. He was bored, mostly, he told them with a depreciating laugh, and was glad he'd finally met some people his own age in this town full of retirees and stuffed shirts. He promised to take Marianne out onto the lake when her ankle healed.

For someone who was staying in one of the lakeside mansions, he didn't seem at all bothered by the Dashwoods' cramped apartment. He even made Greta laugh, which was almost unprecedented and possibly a sign of the apocalypse.

He left once he was satisfied that Marianne was comfortable. Less than ten minutes later, Marianne was checking her text messages with a smile.

Greta exchanged a knowing look with Elliott.

Hours later, when Abby had arrived home, Jack returned with a bag full of boxes from the noodle bar in Whitwell, a new bottle of Tylenol, a proper ice pack, a selection of DVDs, and a single extravagant red velvet cupcake that he presented to Marianne with a wide smile.

Marianne was charmed.

She wasn't the only one, Elliott thought, as Abby's delighted laugh echoed throughout the apartment.

***

Elliott spent the night in Marianne's bed.

"Is he still here?" Greta whispered from the top bunk.

"I think so." If he listened carefully, Elliott could still hear a movie playing faintly from the living room. He didn't want to listen too closely, just in case.

"It was pretty cool, Elliott," Greta confessed in a whisper. "Marianne slipped and fell, and then this guy just sweeps in from nowhere, making sure she's okay, and then he lifted her up like it was something out of a *movie*." She made a small noise of disgust that didn't entirely cover her awe. "Not a movie *I* would watch. Like, a *dumb* movie."

"Obviously."

"But it was still pretty cool," she admitted. "He's pretty cool."

Elliott wanted to believe it. He wanted to believe that Jack's Porsche didn't tell an entire story of its own: one where the Dashwoods were as good as invisible to people like him, to the people in the big houses on the other side of the lake, because they didn't have Henry's money anymore. It was hard to remember that not everyone was like the Family. That old money didn't always mean closed doors. Plenty of times it did though. There was no greater sin to some of these people than having money and then *not* having it.

Elliott wanted to believe that Jack was better than that. Marianne deserved someone better.

He thought again of Ned. He thought of Francesca, her face contorted with outrage when she'd busted them together: *"Oh my god! You dirty little gold-digging whore!"*

Elliott swallowed, a hot lick of anger flaring in his chest. If anyone ever said that to Marianne . . . He cut the thought off before he could finish it.

Jesus. Not everyone was like that. Not everyone was the Family. And Jack seemed like a decent guy. He was clearly head over heels for Marianne already, and he hadn't even blinked when he'd seen the apartment. Not everyone was poisonous.

"Elliott?" Greta whispered.

"Yeah?"

"I really miss Dad." It spilled out of her like a confession, like something she thought was secret, was too shameful to admit. All those sharp edges Greta honed had never been more fragile.

"I miss him too, Greta." Elliott closed his stinging eyes briefly. "I'm going to miss him every day, I think." Their loss was the same, but in some ways it was incomparable. Greta was thirteen, still a kid. She still needed their dad in a way that maybe Elliott didn't. Except... An aching breath shuddered out of him. "I feel so little, you know? Like how am I supposed to figure stuff out without Dad? If I get it wrong, who's supposed to help me?"

Greta made a small, sad noise that tore at his heart.

"But we're going to figure things out together," Elliott said, his voice wavering a little. "You and me, and Marianne and Mom."

"I know," Greta whispered. "It's stupid, but who's gonna walk me down the aisle when I get married? *If* I get married. I don't have to. Because marriage is dumb. Fuck the patriarchy."

"Fuck it," Elliott agreed, but he'd seen Greta eyeing Barbie bridal sets in Target not *that* many years ago. "But if that's something you want one day, then I could do it. If you want."

Greta was silent for a long while.

"Okay," she finally whispered back through the darkness. "Who's going to walk you down the aisle though?"

"You and Mar," Elliott said.

"Can I wear a suit?"

A smile tugged at Elliott's mouth. "Of course you can."

"Good." She sighed, and Elliott heard her sheets rustling. "Goodnight, Elliott."

"Goodnight, Greta."

His sisters' room was darker than the living room. There was no play of lights on the ceiling from outside. Their window was small, and the curtains were tugged closed. A thin sliver of light spilled through a tiny gap, lying across the floor like the blade of a knife. It was enough to catch Elliott's gaze, but not enough to illuminate the room.

From outside he could hear the movie playing softly and the occasional low murmur of voices that confirmed Jack was still there.

Elliott hoped that Marianne knew what she was doing.

***

Elliott slept later than usual the next day without the sunlight to wake him. When he finally stumbled outside into the kitchen, still dragging himself awake, it was to find Marianne sitting propped up on the folded-out couch, a store-bought coffee in her hands, and her sprained ankle elevated.

"What time's'it?" Elliott mumbled.

"Almost nine," Marianne said. "Mom's downstairs in the store, and Greta left for school ages ago. Welcome to the land of the living."

"It's over-rated," Elliott said. "Where'd you get that coffee?"

"Jack," she said, raising the cup to her mouth and smiling at Elliott over the rim.

"Huh." Elliott dragged his fingers through his hair. "And what time did he leave?"

"Pretty late," Marianne said, her smile growing.

Elliott sat down beside her, the springs wheezing. There were a hundred things he wanted to say to her—

Don't move too fast, Mar.

Be careful.

You don't even know him yet.

—but it was nothing she would hear. He and Marianne were too different. She was reckless where he was guarded. Fearless where he was cautious. If she believed it was love, she'd throw herself into it headfirst. Elliott envied her sometimes. She wasn't afraid to truly live.

Maybe . . .

Maybe when Ned came to Barton Lake, Elliott could borrow some of Marianne's bravery. Maybe he could take a risk for once, and see if there was something there.

Maybe it was time Elliott learned how to live.

CHAPTER 9

Elliott finished his lunchtime shift at the restaurant and headed back toward the apartment. He was halfway down the block in the narrow laneway behind Main Street when an engine revved behind him. He moved over to the edge of the laneway, and Jack's silver Porsche pulled in beside him.

Marianne grinned at him from the passenger window. "Get in, loser," she said cheerfully. "We're going to get waffles!"

Elliott grimaced, uncertain. He was tired and his feet hurt, but waffles did sound good.

Jack leaned across her, an easy smile on his face. "Come on, Elliott. You won't regret it."

"Ellioooooooott!" Greta called from the back seat. "Get in!"

He'd been outvoted, clearly, and his reluctance would not be allowed to stand. Elliott knew when he'd lost the fight. He climbed into the back seat.

Marianne twisted around to smile at him, her eyes bright, and Jack revved the engine of the Porsche again, and they zipped down the laneway.

***

The diner was halfway between Barton Lake and Whitwell, on a curve of the highway that cut through a swathe of woodland. Elliott, who hadn't made it further than the grocery store yet, was strangely taken by the beauty of the landscape. The day was bright, and the air was cool. The diner itself was one of those hokey little places that had gone for a milkshakes-and-bobby-socks retro sort of vibe. The booths were cherry red with white formica tables and chrome napkin dispensers.

Marianne hobbled inside leaning on Jack's arm. She slid into the booth and pulled Jack down beside her. They rested their clasped hands on the surface of the table.

"Ugh," Greta said, sitting down across from them and moving over to make room for Elliott. "I don't even like waffles."

"You don't like anything," Marianne reminded her.

"You'll like these waffles," Jack promised. "These waffles are life changing. These waffles are the only things worth coming to Barton Lake for."

"Hey!" Marianne exclaimed.

"Well, they were." Jack quickly leaned in to kiss her.

"Ugh." Greta looked up as the waitress approached, and held out her hand for a menu. "Thank you!"

She opened the menu, set it on the table as a barrier, and ducked down behind it. Elliott reached out and scruffed her hair. She narrowed her eyes at him, and then scowled at the menu.

"How was work?" Jack asked, apparently unfazed by Greta's behavior.

That was probably a good yardstick to measure him by, Elliott thought. He had a sudden flash of memory: Greta haranguing Ned in the kitchen of Norland Park for not being able to beat an egg, and how Ned had enjoyed the way she'd needled him. It made him wonder what it might have been like to sit in a diner booth with Ned, leaning against him the way Marianne was against Jack.

"Work was good," Elliott said. He looked at his menu. "What did you guys do today?"

Marianne beamed at Jack. "We just hung around the apartment and watched movies and stuff."

"Best day ever." Jack put an arm around her.

"You guys make me want to puke." Greta glared at them over the top of her menu, and then brightened as the waitress returned. "Can I get the Nutella Banana Boat, please, and a strawberry milkshake?"

"That sounds disgusting," Elliott said.

"Oooh!" Greta exclaimed. "Look, everyone! Elliott's about to order the blandest and most boring thing on the menu, because you are what you eat!"

Elliott froze.

Just a joke.

He knew it was just a joke, but maybe it hit a little too close for comfort. He forced a smile and scanned the menu. "You know what? I'll have the Nutella Banana boat as well. And a black coffee."

"*That's* how it's done," Greta said, and raised her hand for a high five.

Elliott raised his eyebrows at her—*A high five? Really?*—and passed his menu back to the waitress.

Marianne hummed over her choices for a while, and then declared Jack could order for her. He did so with a good-natured smile.

They talked while they waited for their order. Greta complained about her History teacher, who was also her homeroom teacher, and, apparently, an entire bag of dicks. Elliott let her vent, and wondered if it was something he'd have to mention to Abby. Greta was the sort of kid who would happily let her grades tank out of spite. She'd always been the smartest out of all of them, but if she wasn't challenged by her schoolwork, she had no fucks to give. Henry and Abby had never cared about grades, but it frustrated Elliott because Greta could so easily ace every subject. She just didn't bother.

They talked about the few people they'd met around town. Jack knew Paula and John, and he'd been into the shop before.

"So, you guys work there now," he said. "How is it even still open? Like, how does it turn a profit?"

"That's one of life's eternal mysteries," Marianne said. "Except you'd be surprised by the number of people who buy tarot cards. I sold three packs in a single day last week. You wouldn't think there'd be three people in a town this size who suddenly needed to buy tarot cards, right?"

"It's probably witchcraft," Greta said. "Are we considering the possibility that all of that shit is *real*, and John is a warlock, and he's making blood sacrifices under the full moon to keep the shop solvent?" She grinned at Jack. "Do you get a lot of missing virgins in town?"

"Not that I'm aware of."

"That's exactly the sort of thing an accomplice would say," Greta said.

Jack blinked at her. "I'm an accomplice now?"

"It's probably a town-wide conspiracy." Greta shrugged. "Sorry. You're guilty by association."

"Seems fair," Jack said with a nod. "So, who else have you met? I probably don't know that many people since I only come here for the summers. And mostly I only meet my aunt's stuffy neighbors." He rolled his eyes. "Like that Brandon woman."

"Oh, we know her!" Marianne said. "She seems..."

"Abrupt," Elliott said.

"She's a—*ugh*," Jack said. "She's a total killjoy. And she's always been like that. Way before she lost her leg."

Elliott felt a jolt of surprise. He thought of Colonel Brandon's stiff gait, and the way she held herself so particularly. He thought of the lines radiating out from her tightly-pressed lips, and the tension she carried in her.

"She lost her leg?" Greta was wide-eyed.

"Afghanistan or something." Jack looked slightly abashed. "I mean, she's a veteran, and obviously I respect that, but it doesn't give her a pass on being an asshole, right?"

"Right," Marianne echoed, and looked to Elliott for his agreement.

He was saved from having to answer by the arrival of their food.

***

Jack watched as Greta helped Marianne to the bathroom, and then dragged his finger through the remains of the powdered sugar on his plate. "So this is where you give me the shovel talk, right?"

Elliott considered the question for a moment.

It was only teasing, but Elliott had never been comfortable with the idea that either Marianne or Greta needed a male family member to metaphorically sign off on their choice of partner. Okay, so Greta was only thirteen, but last year back in Massachusetts her class had held a dance, and she'd actually been invested enough to go—Elliott had suspected she'd only gone for the shock value. Greta Dashwood doing something normal? The horror! So a boy had turned up on the doorstep. His father had driven them to the dance. The father had waited in the car.

"So, um, my dad says I'm supposed to introduce myself to your dad?"

the boy had said, skinny and anxious.

"*Why?*" Greta had asked bluntly. She'd strapped her corsage to her wrist aggressively, then grabbed the boy by the hand and dragged him toward the waiting car. "*Bye, Mom! Bye, Dad! I'll try not to get pregnant!*"

Henry Dashwood had raised his daughters to make their own decisions. He hadn't been their keeper. And neither was Elliott, now that Henry was gone.

He shrugged. "Do you like Marianne?"

"Yes. Very much." Jack smiled and shook his head. "I can't even believe how lucky I am right now. I *love* Marianne."

"Then that's all that matters."

"I won't hurt her," Jack said, his smile fading. He looked earnest. "I want you to know that. She isn't like anyone I've ever met before. She's incredible."

"I think she thinks you're pretty incredible yourself."

Jack's smile was back, as bright as before.

The waitress came over and set the bill down on the table.

Jack reached for it before Elliott could. "No, this was my treat."

He left a generous tip.

***

"We were right to come here," Abby said later that night, sitting with Elliott on the couch. Greta was at the table, working on her homework. Marianne was sitting outside on the steps, texting back and forth with Jack even though it had barely been an hour since she'd seen him. "We made the right choice."

Elliott wasn't sure it had been a choice at all, but he nodded.

It was good to see Abby smiling again.

"Marianne looks like I did when I met your father," Abby said. "You can see it lighting her up from the inside." She sighed wistfully. "I can remember exactly what it felt like. Just a single touch, or a glance, and suddenly my skin was tingling all over." She laughed. "Like I'd swallowed a bath bomb!"

"Gross," Greta said from the table without looking up.

"It's quick," Elliott said softly.

Abby clapped a hand over Elliott's knee and jiggled his leg. "You worry too much, Elliott!"

Elliott didn't know if Abby was referring to the Marianne and Jack situation specifically, or if it was just a general observation.

He gave a low hum in response that Abby might take as agreement, and then got up and headed into the kitchen.

He poured himself a glass of water from the jug in the refrigerator, and drank it leaning up against the counter. His gaze was caught by something sitting by a stack of paperwork, half hidden under the loaf of bread. He moved over to extricate it.

The cracked worry stone from the shop.

He picked it up and carried it back into the living room. "What's this doing up here?" he asked.

"Oh." Abby blinked at the stone. "John was going to toss it out, and Marianne said you liked it. Nobody's going to buy a broken worry stone."

Elliott rubbed his thumb over the crack, soothing himself with its familiar flaw. "I guess I'll keep it then."

***

Elliott woke up late that night in time to hear the front door snicking closed. He climbed out of bed, dragging his comforter with him, and opened the door. Marianne was sitting on the back steps in her pajamas, face illuminated in the glow of the small flame as she lit a joint. Elliott wasn't sure where she'd gotten it, but he suspected John was involved.

Abby and Henry had always been liberal when it came to pot, and Elliott was no stranger to getting high.

He wrapped his comforter around his shoulders and sat down on the steps beside Marianne. She tugged a corner of the comforter around herself and passed him the joint.

They sat in silence for a while, handing it back and forth and getting pleasantly buzzed.

"Did you ever want to be a different person?" Marianne asked.

"I don't know. Maybe." It would have been better, he sometimes thought, to be as fearless as Marianne, as hungry for new experiences, but that wasn't the way he was wired. "Why? Who would you want to be if you could be someone else?"

Marianne gave him the side eye.

"What?"

She laughed. "You know what every teacher I ever had used to tell me?" She pulled her mouth into a grimace. "Oh, a Dashwood. You must be Elliott's sister. I expect great things from you, Miss Dashwood!"

Elliott snorted.

Marianne took the joint back and inhaled. She held the smoke in her lungs for as long as she could. When she spoke again, her voice was strained. "You were a hard act to follow."

"Every time they made us do art in school, I used to get the teacher hanging over my shoulder, like they were waiting for me to do something amazing."

"You should call Ned," Marianne said, and then, in response to his blank look: "Ned Ferrars."

"I know which Ned. It's not like I'm drowning in Neds. How many do you think I know?"

"I don't know." Marianne knocked their shoulders together. "Maybe you've got an entire Grindr profile set up where you only hook up with guys called Ned. You might have a Ned kink."

"I don't have a Ned kink." Elliott rolled his eyes. "Anyway, I don't need to call him."

"You don't need to," Marianne agreed, "but you *should.*"

"Why should I?"

"Because!" Marianne exclaimed, her eyes bright. "Because it's so incredible to be in love! And we could be in love together! Like, at the same time, not with each other, because *ew*. That's some *Game of Thrones* Lannister bullshit right there."

"I don't need to be in love, Mar," Elliott said.

"But you're sad," Marianne said. "And I wish you weren't. I want you to be happy too. I mean, it hasn't been long since Dad died, but it's okay to be happy now, right? Isn't it?" She looked suddenly worried.

"It's okay," Elliott said. "And I am happy. I'm happy that you're happy."

"That's a bullshit answer, Elliott. No offence, but that's bullshit."

"It's not bullshit." Elliott adjusted the comforter. "And you don't have to feel guilty about being happy. Dad would want you to be happy."

"He'd want you to be happy too."

"Yeah, but we're different people, Mar." He gazed down into the soft darkness of the back yard. "You throw your whole heart into everything. You always have, and I think that's amazing, but that's not who I am. I can't just pick up the phone and call Ned."

"What's the worst thing that could happen if you did?"

Elliott laughed. "Um, he might *answer*!"

God. Elliott could just imagine the six million ways that could go horribly wrong.

Hey, Ned. This is Elliott. Elliott Dashwood. Remember? We last saw each other when we had each other's dicks in our hands and your sister screamed that I was a gold digging whore. So, how are things?

And as ludicrous as that was, he knew that if she were in his shoes, Marianne would have made a call like that without any shame at all. Marianne had this knack of taking the most embarrassing things she'd ever done and laughing at them. When other people laughed too, she was already laughing with them. Elliott had never gotten the hang of that. Elliott was the sort of person who lay awake at night, still feeling the sting of humiliation from being six years old and accidentally calling his teacher Mom.

And maybe it was more than the way he was wired.

Maybe Elliott was working hard enough at dealing with his grief that he didn't need anything else to wrestle with right now. He was happy that Marianne was happy, but Elliott couldn't juggle a bunch of different emotions at once. He just couldn't. He needed to concentrate on practicalities right now, and on coming to terms with the loss of his dad before he even thought about something as new and terrifying as love.

Marianne would tell him it didn't work like that. She'd tell him that love didn't come when it was convenient. Love was a force of nature, a hurricane, not a bus you waited for, your timetable in hand. You battened down in a storm, though. You waited it out in the cellar until it passed. You didn't open up the windows and let it in.

Whatever Elliott's feelings were for Ned Ferrars, he was waiting them out. That was the only safe thing to do.

"We should get some fairy lights," Marianne said at last. "It would be so pretty out here with fairy lights."

Elliott took the joint off her, glad for the change in subject. "Yeah, maybe."

"Can we afford fairy lights?" she asked. "How poor are we?"

"We are poor enough that we shouldn't be spending money on fairy lights."

Marianne tilted her head. "We should get John to buy us fairy lights. Brother John, not cousin John."

"I don't think we should bother him for a while."

Marianne huffed. "Oh, please. He's got a gazillion dollars. He can buy us some fucking fairy lights."

"Or maybe we should play nice until we have to hit him up for things that actually matter," Elliott countered.

"This is your problem right here." She knocked him with her shoulder. "You think fairy lights don't matter."

"Yeah." Elliott snorted. "*That's* my problem."

"I bet Jack will buy me some fairy lights." Marianne leaned against him. "I love him so much."

"Yeah. He's pretty great."

Marianne smiled. "I bet he'd buy me all the fairy lights in the world, and then everything would be beautiful forever."

Elliott put his arm around her. He didn't think for a second that Marianne needed fairy lights to make the world seem beautiful forever. She just needed to keep looking at it the way she always had. And maybe, when he was ready to face a hurricane, he could borrow some of that incredible optimism that lit her up from the inside.

CHAPTER 10

Sunlight glittered on the surface of the lake. Elliott leaned on the railing of the verandah at the Boathouse and watched Jack's tiny sailboat dart across the water. The white sail shone brightly in the sun. Elliott had stood on the shore with Marianne half an hour ago as she'd waited for Jack to arrive and collect her from the other side of the lake. He wondered how long they'd be out on the water. Time probably passed differently for them in their bubble.

In the two weeks since Marianne had sprained her ankle, Jack had been a constant presence at her side. Elliott hadn't heard her laugh much since their dad's death; it was good to hear it again now. And while two weeks was barely the blink of an eye to Elliott, to Marianne it must have felt like a lifetime. She and Jack were both equally besotted with one another.

Elliott squinted into the sunlight and wondered what they were talking about out there. He tried to imagine himself sitting in a boat with someone—with Ned, because why not?—and what they might talk about. He and Ned had never really talked though, had they?

John appeared beside him and leaned on the railing. "It looks beautiful out there today."

Elliott nodded.

"Thinking of someone you'd like to take out on the water?" John asked, and spoke again before Elliott could think of a response. "Or worrying Marianne's getting in over her head?"

Elliott smiled wryly. "Maybe a bit of the second one."

"She's just like Abby was at that age," John said, staring out at the lake and past the last two decades. "And I think that turned out okay, didn't it?"

It was a hard thing to consider, because the memories of his father were still too painful, but Elliott knew John was right. Henry and Abby got a little over twenty years of happiness. That was more that some people got in a lifetime. Henry might have been taken from them too soon—God, *way* too soon—but John was right.

"Yeah," he said at last. "I think it did."

John smiled.

"Jack seems like a good guy," Elliott said.

John nodded. "He's spent most his summers here since he was a kid. Not that his aunt associates with us common townies. Stick the size of the Sears Tower up her ass, that one. But Jack has always been friendly."

Elliott watched the small boat cutting through the glittering water.

"Now," John said, nudging Elliott with his elbow, "help me get the grill fired up, and I'll make you the best tofu burger you've ever had."

"That bar is set pretty low, John."

John's laughter was booming.

***

Marianne and Jack spent the following weekend at a hotel. The tiny apartment felt strangely spacious without her. Greta took advantage of not having to share a bedroom; Elliott woke up on Sunday morning to the tinny strains of Greta's music coming from behind her door. Elliott showered and dressed. The music was louder when he left the bathroom. Greta's door was open, and Elliott looked inside. Greta was rooting around in a suitcase, flinging clothes behind her onto the floor.

"What are you doing?"

Greta twisted around, scowling. "Looking for my shirt!"

"Which one?"

"My 'Dostoevsky is my brostoevsky' shirt."

"Greta, did you bring it?"

Greta huffed. "What?"

"I haven't seen you wear it since we moved." Elliott met her worried gaze. "Are you sure you didn't forget it?"

"No!" Greta shook her head. "It's one of my favorite shirts. I wouldn't—" Her face fell. "Oh."

"What?"

Greta slammed the suitcase shut. "It was in the laundry basket. That's the last place I saw it. I left it in Massachusetts, Elliott." Her lower lip trembled.

"We'll get you another one."

Greta dropped her gaze to the floor. "It's just a dumb shirt."

"Yeah, well guess who got a paycheck last night? Go online and find the shirt."

"Elliott . . ." Greta met his gaze. She sniffed. "That's dumb. That's a dumb thing to spend your paycheck on."

"Order the shirt, Greta," Elliott said. "You can pay me back by helping out in the store this morning, since Marianne's decided to take the weekend off."

"You're just jealous some hot guy isn't sexing you up in a hotel room," Greta shot back.

"Please don't ever say 'sexing you up' about anyone. Ever again. And I'm not jealous."

Mostly.

"Right." Greta huffed. "You're not jealous at all. I don't know what's stopping you. You're cute. You could get laid."

"And I am not having this conversation with my thirteen-year-old sister," Elliott announced, and turned and headed for the kitchen. "Do you want French toast?"

"Yes!" Greta called after him. "With extra cinnamon!"

"I *know*!"

Elliott got to work in the kitchen. By the time Greta was showered and dressed, Abby had emerged from her room. The three of them ate together, crowded around the tiny table, and then Greta followed Elliott down the interior stairs into the store.

"Does John really make a living selling all this weird stuff?" Greta asked, poking around at a display of essential oils in pretty little bottles.

"I think Paula makes all the money in their relationship."

Greta hummed. "She's really keen about selling that land. Like, she wants someone to build a resort on it or something. If you had the choice between like here and the Ritz-Carlton at Half Moon Bay or something, would you really come here?"

"It's nice here." Elliott turned on the register.

"Is it Ritz-Carlton nice though?" Greta asked, waggling her eyebrows.

"Since when are you pro-Ritz-Carlton?"

"Paula has one of their brochures in her office. I read it when Mom and I visited. She wants to build something like that here. She's the one making the comparison, not me. If it was me, I'd knock down all the fancy houses on the north side of the lake and build an eco-resort."

"You don't even know what an eco-resort is."

"It's like a regular resort, but there's no golf course." Greta shrugged. "Probably. And it would have yoga classes and everything would smell of patchouli. I don't know. I bet John could run the gift shop though."

"I bet he could."

Greta lifted up a little box of worry dolls and inspected them. "Do these really work?"

Elliott raised his eyebrows. "Are you asking me that for real?"

"No." Greta set the bright little box back down on the shelf. "I guess if they did, people would make mattresses out of them. How creepy would that be?" She poked at a crystal wolf. "So what do you and Marianne actually do when you're 'working'?" she asked, complete with air quotes.

"Well, sometimes we unlock the front door so actual customers can come in and buy things." Elliott dug into the basket of worry stones on the counter, unconsciously searching for the one with the cracked surface until he realized what he was doing and remembered it was upstairs.

Greta snorted, but moved forward to unlock the door and flip the sign to 'open'. "And now what?"

"And now we stand around and wait in case someone actually shows up. And we play snap with the display pack of tarot cards. We're working on a system of playing poker as well, but we keep confusing ourselves with the Major Arcana. At some point we should get some actual playing cards instead."

"Cool," Greta said. "I'm down to play snap with Death and the Hanged Man."

The morning passed easily. They played snap, served the few customers that made their way into the store, and swapped out the meditation CD for a Led Zeppelin one they found in one of the drawers behind the counter. Greta amused herself by rearranging all the little crystal animals to make it look like they were fleeing from one of the wizards. Elliott left her in charge when he went upstairs to make sandwiches for lunch. When he got back, she was slumped on the stool behind the counter, playing a game on her phone.

Just after one, the bells on door jangled, and Colonel Brandon stepped inside. She walked stiffly up to the counter.

"Hi," Elliott said.

"I, um, I need to reorder this DVD," she said, and set the case down on the counter.

"Oh," Elliott said. "Is there a problem?"

Her mouth turned down at the corners, and she snapped the case open. The shattered remains of the DVD slithered out onto the counter.

"Apparently I didn't find it as relaxing as it promised I would."

Greta's eyes grew wide with delight.

"And you want to reorder that one?" Elliott asked. "Or do you want to try a different one?"

Colonel Brandon glanced at the wire display rack of DVDs and then back to Elliott. "I don't know. I was hoping your sister would be here to give me some advice?"

"Marianne's not working today, sorry." Elliott looked down at the pieces of shattered DVD again. "I don't really know that much about yoga."

"Oh." Colonel Brandon cleared her throat. "Will she be working tomorrow?"

"She's supposed to be," Elliott said.

"She can be a flake," Greta added.

Colonel Brandon looked at Greta in surprise, as though noticing her for the first time.

"I'm Greta," Greta said, and stuck out her hand. "The other sister."

Colonel Brandon shook her hand, her expression softening for the first time since she'd entered the store. "My name is Deanna. It's nice to meet you, Greta."

"You too," Greta said.

Colonel Brandon shifted her weight awkwardly. "Well, um, I'll stop in tomorrow and see if she's here."

"Okay," Elliott said.

Colonel Brandon scooped up the broken pieces of the DVD, dropped them back into the case, and squeezed it shut again. She slipped it into her jacket pocket and walked awkwardly back toward the door again. The bells jingled and danced as she pulled the door open.

It closed slowly behind her.

"Wow," Greta said in the silence that followed her departure. "She's a weird one."

"Says you," Elliott said. "Who isn't weird at all."

Greta rolled her eyes. "It just means I'm an *expert*."

They went back to playing snap.

"Elliott?" Greta asked after a few more rounds.

"Mmm?"

"Are you looking forward to Ned coming to visit?"

"He's not coming to visit." Elliott turned a card over. The Empress stared at him haughtily. "He's coming to look at some property Paula wants to sell."

"And you being here has nothing to do with that at all?" Greta pressed.

"Why would it?"

The next card was the Moon. She was a woman too. Elliott liked her more than the Empress. She had been drawn with a gentler cast to her features.

Abby had a deck of tarot cards somewhere. She'd gone though a few periods in her life where she'd liked to read them at least once a day. She'd tried to explain to Elliott once that she didn't believe the tarot told her fortune, as such, but that the cards offered guidance to someone receptive to it. It was the same as palmistry, or reading tea leaves, or checking her horoscope every morning. Elliott had never been particularly interested, but Marianne had gotten into it for a while. She'd done spreads for all her friends from school. Marianne could probably tell him exactly what it meant to draw the Moon after the Empress.

"He's nice," Greta said at last. "Ned is."

"Yeah, he is. Doesn't mean he's coming to see me though."

"Doesn't mean he isn't," Greta countered. "Have you asked him?"

"No."

Greta snorted.

Elliott idly shuffled the deck of tarot cards. "What?"

"I was just thinking that if we put you and Marianne together, you'd make a perfectly well balanced human being."

"Again with the stone throwing." Elliott pulled a card out of the deck and almost laughed. The Lovers. Of course. "What's the view like from inside that glass house of yours?"

"My threats to stab people are exaggerated at best," Greta said with an evil smirk.

"You be sure to let your future defense team know that."

"I'll also tell them not to call you as a character witness."

"That is a very good idea." Elliott cut the deck and turned over the top card.

Death stared back at him.

Marianne would probably have something to say about that as well. The Lovers, followed by Death. Well, everything was followed by Death, Elliott supposed. And some things were preceded by it, like uprooting their lives and somehow ending up right here, in this dinky little shop in a tiny little town in northern California, surrounded by incense smoke and crystals.

They closed the shop at four, and headed down Main Street to see if the coffee place was still open. Elliott bought Greta a hot chocolate and a slice of coconut sponge, and ordered himself a coffee. A boy waiting at the counter for his order shuffled his feet.

"H-hey," he said at last. "Greta, right? You're the new girl."

"That's me," Greta said, not even cracking a smile. "Shiny and new."

"You're in honors History," the boy said. "I sit behind you. It's Mitchell. That's my name. Mitchell."

Greta blinked at him.

"Um," Mitchell said, and Elliott could almost see him desperately clutching at any straws he could. "Did you do your homework yet?"

"You can't copy off me."

Mitchell turned red. "Oh, no, I . . . I wasn't going to?"

"Good," Greta said, narrowing her eyes. "I'm glad we got that settled."

Five minutes later as they walked back toward the apartment, Elliott said, "You know that kid was trying to ask you out, right?"

Greta wrinkled her nose and gave him a sideways look. "What? No he wasn't. He wanted to copy my homework!"

"Pretty sure he didn't."

"Well, that's dumb." Greta scowled. "Boys are dumb."

But she wore a thoughtful expression all the way back to the apartment.

***

Marianne and Jack's whirlwind romance was fast, intense, and ripped the air from her lungs. When Elliott got home from the restaurant on Sunday night, Marianne was sitting on the top step waiting for him, wrapped in a comforter and smoking a joint.

"He's gone," she said. Her eyes were red-rimmed from crying. "He's gone back to New York."

Elliott sat down beside her and put his arm around her shoulders.

"I mean, he'll be *back*," Marianne said with a shaky laugh. "Of course he will! But I already miss him."

He'll be back.

She said it a few times over the next few days. She lived and died by the pinging text message notifications on her phone, each one buoying her up again and rebuilding her shaken happiness.

He'll be back.

He's busy.

He loves me.

Abby was in total agreement. "Oh, Mar. The way Jack looks at you, of course he's in love with you. A blind man could see it."

Greta looked worriedly at Elliott whenever Marianne or Abby talked about it, as though she were waiting for him to say something to contradict them. Elliott didn't. Whatever was going on with Jack, it hadn't been an act with Marianne. Elliott hoped he was a good enough judge of character to be sure of that.

But love wasn't all encompassing, was it? There was love, but there was also work, or school, or day-to-day life. The bubble had to burst sooner or later. Didn't it? Henry and Abby and their great romance were the exception to the rule, Elliott had always thought. And, even then behind all the grand gestures, they'd had something smaller, quieter, but also stronger. And that small, quiet thing, that certain bond between them, that was what Elliott thought of when he thought of love. Not sailboats or serenades, not poems or presents. Just two people who looked at one another and thought: *yes*.

He hoped, now that Marianne and Jack's bubble had burst, that the *yes* still somehow remained.

CHAPTER 11

Elliott arrived home from an afternoon shift at the restaurant to find Ned Ferrars sitting at the small kitchen table. Elliott had been half expecting it, but he still froze for a moment in surprise before he remembered how to breathe again. Ned looked out of place in the poky little apartment, sitting there uncomfortably as though he was trying to take up less room than his body usually required. He was dressed more casually than Elliott had seen him before, in jeans and a well-fitted henley, and yet he still managed to look overdressed in comparison to his surroundings.

An expression Elliott couldn't read flashed across Ned's face when their gazes met, and then Ned smiled slightly. "Elliott. Hi."

"Hi." Elliott wished he were wearing something that didn't smell quite so strongly of garlic sauce.

So did Abby, apparently.

She fluttered toward him, her patchwork skirt swirling as she moved. "Go and have a shower and get changed, and then we're taking Ned on a tour of Barton Lake before we go to the Boathouse for dinner."

Elliott nodded dumbly. He grabbed some clean clothes from the stack he kept beside the television and headed for the shower.

Thought about drowning himself to save the awkwardness that was sure to come. It was stupid. The time for shyness had passed, surely. He'd had the guy's dick in his hand, for fuck's sake.

A burst of laughter—Abby's—carried above the noise of the shower. It was weirdly embarrassing to realize that the walls were so thin here, and the rooms so small, that if he could hear his mom laughing, then Ned could hear the spray of the shower. Could hear the way it changed pitch when Elliott angled his body into it, or cupped his hands to splash his face.

Elliott grimaced.

He was thinking about Ned thinking about him showering.

Yeah, too weird.

Elliott tried to concentrate on scrubbing the smell of garlic out of his skin, and not think about Ned sitting in the tiny apartment.

Except what was Ned doing here? Had he really flown all the way across the continent just to look at some lakeside land? Maybe. Elliott had no idea what Ned actually did. Something to do with construction or property development, whatever the hell that entailed. Maybe this was standard practice for property developers? Maybe he wasn't here to see Elliott at all.

Until he thought that, Elliott hadn't realized how much hope he'd somehow stacked onto the idea.

Stupid.

Thinking around in circles wasn't going to solve anything. It wasn't going to cause a seismic shift anywhere in Elliott's consciousness that would let him suddenly see the truth. He didn't have enough information to decide exactly what was going on here and what it meant.

He could . . . he could *ask*?

Elliott snorted.

No. No, because asking was an act of vulnerability. It was showing his belly, baring his throat. It was opening himself to the prospect of being hurt, and Elliott wasn't courageous like that. He wasn't reckless. He wasn't Marianne.

Standing in the shower with the spray hitting his shoulders, Elliott had never been more starkly aware of his own deficiencies. He could just ask, but at the same time, asking was the most unthinkable thing in the world.

And for what? He didn't know Ned Ferrars. Not really.

Elliott sighed and twisted the shower off. He dried himself and dressed, dragged his fingers through his damp hair to at least give it some vague style, and then stared at himself in the mirror until he worked up the courage to leave the bathroom. It took longer than he wanted to admit.

***

Abby drove on their impromptu tour of Barton Lake.

"The girls are meeting us at the Boathouse," she announced. "It's just us! Do you want to sit up front with me, Ned, or back there with Elliott?"

Ned sat in the front. Elliott was half glad. Not just because it would have felt weird to have Abby driving them around like a chauffeur, but because this way he was spared at least a little awkwardness. There was a slight sting of disappointment attached to Ned's decision, though. Did Ned not want to sit next to him?

The day was bright: perfect weather for showing Barton Lake's picture-postcard beauty.

Elliott sat back and looked out the window, trying to pretend Ned wasn't right there, and listened to his mother's commentary on the things they passed. He had lived here for weeks now, but there was still a lot of the town he hadn't seen. Abby had picked a route that did a circuit of the lake, going past those huge summer homes that Elliott had only ever seen from the verandah of the Boathouse before.

Colonel Brandon lived over here somewhere, behind one of those sets of ornate gates. So did Sophia Smith, Jack's aunt. And so, once upon a time, had Henry Dashwood, if only for a summer or two. Elliott wondered which house his father had lived in with his first wife and with John. He wondered what a breath of fresh air Abby must have been in John's life, but how his parents' divorce must have soured those memories for him.

In the driver's seat, Abby effused about the wildflowers that grew along the lakeshore: the delicate purple ground irises, the bright yellow monkey flowers, and the burnt-orange wind poppies. Ned nodded along, craning his head occasionally at things that caught his attention as they passed.

Their route around the lake brought them back onto Pier Lane at last, and Abby pulled into the driveway at the Boathouse. The afternoon was softening into dusk, and since Elliott has last visited, someone had strung up fairy lights in the shrubs that lined the driveway. It was pretty. Elliott glanced at Ned as they walked toward the entrance, and wondered if that was the sort of detail he noticed.

Would he be impressed by the small, quiet charms of the Boathouse and of Barton Lake, or was he the sort of person who wouldn't notice them at all?

There was something of a crowd at the Boathouse this evening. John and Paula and the girls, Marianne and Greta, the other members of the Barton Lake Tourist Board, and whichever Barton Lake residents Paula had considered necessary to impress an East Coast property developer.

Elliott found a spot by the railing and watched as Paula, in a pair of stilettos as sharp as her suit, escorted Ned from group to group. Ned's smile seemed polite but reserved. He glanced at Elliott more than once, his expression unreadable in those moments, and Elliott hated the way each glance caused a burst of nervous energy to thrum through him.

Marianne sought him out, her eyes bright. "Ned looks good," she said, pressing a glass of wine into Elliott's hand. "Did you guys talk?"

"Not really." Elliott sipped the wine.

Not at all.

Because what were they supposed to talk about?

***

The lights across the lake were glittering when Elliott escaped the party and wandered down to the lakeshore. He was on his second glass of wine, maybe his third. Whatever. He had a pleasant buzz going on, and that's what counted. He walked down to the edge of the water and heard the tiny waves lapping at the shore. When he turned and looked back at the Boathouse, he saw that the verandah was lit up. People were talking and laughing. Soft strains of music drifted down to him, somehow making him feel distant, excluded, although he was the one who'd left.

He stood at the edge of the water, watching the lights reflected on the dark surface of the lake. He had no idea how long he stood there before the crunch of shoes on gravel alerted him to the fact he wasn't alone anymore.

Elliott turned. "Ned." In the low light, he didn't know if he imagined Ned's faint smile or not. "How have you been?"

"Good," Ned said, his voice soft. "You?"

"Good," Elliott echoed, and they stood for a moment in silence.

He remembered how Ned had sat next to him in the old greenhouse back at Norland Park. He remembered how Ned had listened and offered Elliott, a stranger, comfort. He remembered that underneath Ned's slightly pinched exterior was someone who was genuinely warm. A friend in a time when Elliott had needed one. And maybe something a little more than that. Elliott still didn't know that for sure, but that was okay. He didn't need to pin it down and define it yet. Ned was a friend, and that was more than enough.

Except he also remembered the kiss in the greenhouse, and in the kitchen. He remembered the way that it felt almost as though they'd been drawn together like magnets. He remembered the frantic heat that day in his dad's studio. Heat and friction and the smell of paint.

Arousal coiled low in his gut, and then lower still.

"It's been different," he said at last. "This town. The apartment. Everything."

"Good different or bad different?" Ned asked. He wasn't looking at Elliott. He was looking at the lake instead.

"Not bad. John—Mom's cousin John, not Dad's other son John—has been really good to us. The apartment's no Norland Park . . ." He stopped himself and paused for a moment. "It's never going to be *good*, you know? Not how it happened. Not with Dad. That's what makes it hard, I mean. Losing Dad, not losing our money."

"I wouldn't have thought you meant the money," Ned said.

He wouldn't have. The Family would have, and half the northern shore of Lake Barton, from what Elliott knew of them.

The wind whispered in the leaves. An owl gave a mournful call.

"Okay," Elliott said. He swallowed, his throat suddenly dry. "Thank you."

Was this it? Was this the moment? Were they done with the small talk? Elliott wanted to be done with it. He wanted to kiss Ned, to press against him, to stoke the heat building inside him into an inferno. He wanted to be reckless again.

He turned toward Ned, warmth expanding in his chest.

Ned jerked away.

A rush of heat that had nothing to do with arousal flooded

through Elliott. Had he ... had he misread this? God, he had. Clearly he had, given the way Ned was staring at him like he'd suddenly grown a second head.

Elliott's face burned.

Ned had come to Barton Lake to look at a piece of land, not to recapture whatever they'd had between them back in Massachusetts. Had something changed since then, or ...?

Flashes of memory came at him hard and fast: the greenhouse, the kitchen, the studio. Vibrant leaves. Loam. Oil paints and pancake batter. Mouths and skin and the rising heat.

Or had Elliott read too much into it from the start?

God.

The blood roared in his skull. His throat ached.

Ned shifted his weight from foot to foot. He slid his hands into his pockets, and then nodded his head in the direction of the Boathouse. "I should go back. Talk to the locals."

"Yeah," Elliott said, a sour taste rising in his throat as a fresh wave of humiliation hit. He nodded and forced a smile. "Of course, yeah."

He watched Ned walk back to the party.

***

Elliott hadn't known how tightly his unformed hopes had wound themselves around him until they threatened to choke him. He hadn't realized how much he'd been looking forward to seeing Ned Ferrars again—a friend? Something more?—until Ned had come and gone and left an emptiness behind in Elliott. An absence not of the man himself, but of the expectation that Elliott had unknowingly attached to him. All this time telling himself that Ned was just a friend ... a part of Elliott must never have truly believed it if it hurt to discover it was actually true.

"So?" Marianne asked, curling up with him on the couch the night after Ned left. "You talked, right? You and Ned?"

"No." Elliott wondered if she had any weed on her.

"I know Paula was stuck to him like a wet Kleenex the night of the party, but after," Marianne said. "Like, the next day or whatever."

The next day.

Elliott had gone to work downstairs, and then at the restaurant. He'd thought of Ned. Thought of him pacing around the lakeshore with Paula, looking at a parcel of land overgrown with a tangle of weeds and bracken, and seeing past that into some structure that didn't exist yet, but might one day. Elliott's mind had constructed fantasies as he'd worked: the door would open and Ned would walk in. "Sorry," he'd say. "I had to deal with this property thing first. Can I buy you a drink now, though?"

Except Ned hadn't appeared, and Elliott later found out from John that he'd already left. He hadn't even stopped in to say goodbye.

"No," Elliott said to Marianne. "We didn't."

"Oh, Elliott!"

"We weren't a thing," Elliott said woodenly. "I tried to tell you guys back at Norland Park. We were never a thing. We hooked up. We're not *dating*." He tried to laugh at the word, but the sound that came out of him was too uncertain to be mockery. "We didn't . . . He doesn't *owe* me anything."

Marianne's expression was one of disbelief.

This time Elliott did laugh. He reached out and cupped a hand to her cheek. "Oh, Jesus, Mar. You . . . the whole world's a love story to you because you're in love with the whole world, you know? I'm not like you, Mar. I can't see the world the way you do, or the way Mom does. That's not me."

Marianne's eyes shone. She pressed her hand over his and leaned her cheek into it. "But Elliott, you love him."

He somehow kept his voice steady. "Mar, I don't know him."

And that was all there was to it.

***

It took a while for the odd, intrusive thoughts of Ned Ferrars to stop coming. It felt a little like grief, in a strange way. The forgetfulness. The way his brain idly wondered what Ned was doing, or remembered how it had felt to kiss him or get off with him against that terrible painting, before suddenly jolting with surprise when the truth hit him on the heels of those dumb fantasies: *you're nothing to each other. Stop it.*

Elliott wasn't sure how Ned had managed to embed himself so deeply into his subconscious, like he belonged there, when the whole time Elliott had known there was nothing in it. When the hell had any part of him started to believe otherwise? For someone who was adamant he wasn't the same as Marianne, he'd brought this disappointment on himself, hadn't he?

He kept busy with work, and with working out a family budget so that they didn't need to dip into their savings. He started pricing apartments or houses for rent in the local area, quickly realizing they were out of reach on a single income—Marianne's job at the cinema had fallen through when she'd hurt her ankle. He wondered a few times if he should call John Dashwood and ask for money, but things weren't that dire. But also, should he wait for things to be dire? John had promised their dad he'd look after them, and Elliott was tired of being stabbed repeatedly every night by the springs in the mattress of the foldout couch. Wanting a place with his own room and his own bed didn't feel too selfish.

It was almost a relief to be back to focusing on the practicalities of their reduced circumstances. To be budgeting for groceries and gas, and nudging Marianne toward checking out the courses at the local community college—"No, not necessarily for now if you don't want to. But for next year."—and making sure that Greta was doing okay at her new school, and that Abby was keeping busy. Abby was making bead bracelets to sell in the store. Elliott wasn't sure they'd turn enough of a profit to be worth the hours of work she put into each one, but it gave her something to do in her quiet hours apart from miss Henry.

Marianne, now that her ankle had healed, was learning belly dancing with her friend from Whitwell, and had picked up two shifts a week at the cinema on Main Street. She brought home stale popcorn at the end of every shift, and they ate it on the couch and watched TV. She didn't make a lot of money, but every little bit meant they dipped less into their savings.

The weeks passed.

Elliott sensed a shift in the air that was more than the approaching end of summer. They still talked about Henry, but the sharp edges of their loss had been worn away a little. The ache would always remain, probably, but the sting was gone. Henry's light was no longer eclipsed by the darkness of loss. They laughed when they remembered him now.

Very slowly, the Dashwoods were healing.

CHAPTER 12

The bells on the shop door jangled merrily right before closing, and a woman wearing a startling shade of fuchsia wafted inside. Her perfume clashed violently with the jasmine incense Elliott was burning. She was tall and statuesque, made up of the same angles Georgy Kurasov might have painted. Her sharp bob was dyed inky-black. It had been bright red the last time Elliott had seen her.

"Elliott Fucking Dashwood," the woman announced, her voice smoker's-rough. She glared at him over the top of a pair of undoubtedly expensive sunglasses. "How the fuck are you?"

Elliott spilled a tribe of worry dolls all over the counter. "Odette! Holy shit!"

Odette Jennings was a woman of indeterminate age. She liked that phrase, and bullied writers into using it whenever she was being profiled in the arts section of some newspaper or magazine. Elliott had been to her sixtieth birthday party three years ago, though, so he could do the math. Odette was an art dealer. She had a small but ridiculously expensive gallery in SoHo where Henry Dashwood had sold his work exclusively, and had been a family friend since before Elliott could remember.

Elliott rounded the counter and moved forward to give her a hug. "What the hell are you doing here?"

"I got your address off your brother," she said, tugging her sunglasses off. "That man knows nothing about art, by the way. Can you believe he asked me why I couldn't just move Henry's canvases by U-haul? What a fucking philistine."

"That, um . . ." That sounded a lot like John, actually. "Yeah."

Odette's expression softened. "How are you?"

"I'm okay," Elliott said, choosing his words carefully. "I mean, we miss him, you know?"

"Yeah, sweetheart." Odette's eyes shone, and she blinked rapidly. "I know."

"What are you doing here?" Elliott asked her. Barton Lake was a hell of a long way from Odette's usual haunts. She used to complain when she came to visit the Dashwoods at Norland Park that she couldn't sleep properly without the sound of sirens. It was rare enough that Odette made it as far as Massachusetts. Elliott couldn't imagine what the hell she was doing in a small town on the opposite side of the country.

Odette looked smug. "I'm here to make my annual offer for *Abigail in Lamplight.*"

The Naked Blue Lady.

It had been an ongoing joke between Odette and Henry for years, except this time Elliott couldn't raise the ghost of a smile. "No. No way, Odette. You know what that painting means to Mom. She'll never sell it. Especially not now."

"I know that, kiddo," Odette said, her voice more like a growl. "I'm not a fucking idiot. I'm talking about her letting me rent it."

"*Rent* it?"

Odette tapped him on the forearm with a well-manicured talon. "What say we talk about it over dinner? Is there a decent restaurant in this town? My fucking treat."

***

Abby and Odette made an odd pair, walking arm and arm down Main Street toward the restaurant, Odette in her sharply tailored fuchsia pantsuit, and Abby in a patchwork skirt and a cheesecloth tunic. Elliott and his sisters let them walk ahead a little. Abby was chattering like a bird, and Odette was listening to her, head tilted to try to bridge their height disparity; Abby barely came up to Odette's shoulder.

"I can't believe she came all the way here," Marianne said, flashing a bright smile at Elliott.

"I can't believe she left Manhattan at all," Greta said. "Pretty sure that's a sign of the Apocalypse."

Ahead of them, Odette and Abby entered the restaurant.

"Pretty sure *you're* a sign of the Apocalypse," Marianne told Greta fondly, and Greta smirked.

They reached the restaurant, and Elliott held the door open for his sisters. When he got inside, Abby and Odette were already being seated at a table by the window. Elliott followed Marianne and Greta over to them.

"Order whatever you like," Odette said. "The gallery's paying."

Greta reached happily for the menu the server held out for her.

"We don't need your charity, Odette," Abby said, but there was a fond smile on her face.

"This isn't charity. This is a business meeting. Tax deductible. You're the ones doing me a favor."

Elliott doubted that very much, but he knew better than to argue with her.

They ordered their meals.

They didn't talk business at first. Odette asked Greta about her new school, and Greta told her about the water stain on the ceiling panel in her homeroom that looked like Jesus if she squinted at it right. Then she told her about the awful cafeteria food and the particular smell of the school bus, and then, in a more cautious tone altogether, about the art teacher who was really impressed with her drawings.

"Ah," Odette said. "So in five years I'll be exhibiting your work, will I?"

Greta snorted and dug into the complimentary breadsticks. "If I ever figure out my style, maybe."

"Greta's in her 'paint everything black' phase," Abby said with a smile.

"Anger makes me happy," Greta said.

In any other company, Elliott thought wryly, a statement like that might be given the side-eye.

The server brought the meals out and refilled their water glasses.

"So, business," Odette said, stabbing at her fettuccine. "I want to do an exhibit of Henry's pieces. Part retrospective, part homage. And I want *Abigail in Lamplight* to be the centerpiece. It's his best work, and we all know it."

"It's not for sale," Abby said mildly.

"So let me borrow it."

"You're a gallery, not a museum."

"So let me *rent* it," Odette said. "Let me exploit it, basically. *Abigail in Lamplight* will get more people through the door. Even if I can't sell the original, I want to do some merchandise. Prints, postcards, magnets, tote bags—"

Greta almost choked on her water. "Tote bags? Who would want a tote bag with Mom's vulva on it? No offence, Mom."

Abby raised her eyebrows. "I'll have you know my vulva was in incredible shape back then. Before I pushed three of you melon heads out of it."

Elliott resisted the urge to look around and make sure nobody had heard them. Sometimes it was better not to know than to accidentally make eye contact with a traumatized bystander.

"The naked body is nothing to be ashamed of," Marianne said.

Greta wrinkled her nose. "Yeah, but that doesn't mean you should print it on tote bags and take it to Trader Joe's."

"I've always thought my vulva gives off more of a famers' market vibe myself." Abby leaned over and stole a potato wedge off the edge of Greta's plate.

Greta squawked in outrage.

"Getting back on track," Odette said smoothly, "I want you to let me use Abigail in Lamplight for merchandising, and as the focal point of the entire exhibit. It wouldn't be for sale, and I'd pay you a licensing fee."

"What sort of fee?" Elliott asked.

"That's where we negotiate." Odette leveled him with a stare. "I'm prepared to offer either a standard payment up front, or a percentage of profits on the merchandise. This isn't something I've done before, so I don't know what sort of returns we're looking at, but my new assistant Lucien is putting together a few different proposals. I figured I'd make sure you'd actually agree to it before he got too far into the numbers though."

Elliott nodded.

Odette sipped her water and set the glass back down on the table. She left a lipstick stain on the lip of the glass. "I don't need your decision right away. Of course this is something you might want to talk about in private, but I hope you know I value Henry's legacy dearly."

Abby reached out and squeezed her forearm. "Of course we know that, Odette."

"But if you do agree to this," Odette continued, "I'd want you there for the opening. I want you to represent Henry."

Marianne brightened.

"I want to show people his diary entries, his photographs, his family," Odette said. "I want them to know the Henry Dashwood we all did."

Elliott pushed his broccoli florets around his plate with his fork, uncertain. His father had been a wonderful, amazing, and deeply flawed person. A gemstone, roughly cut, with a hundred different facets each reflecting a different thing. Elliott was uncomfortable with the idea that a human being could be reduced to diary entries and photographs—the detritus of a lifetime, not the sum of it. He had no doubt that Odette's love for Henry would shine through in whatever exhibit she put together, but it would never be the full story.

Elliott had never read his father's diaries. Had he ever written about John, and the guilt he'd felt in leaving him? Had he ever actually felt guilt? Elliott loved his father deeply, but he knew the sort of man he was. Impulsive, selfish, always ready to seize the day. What did that feel like to the son he'd left behind?

Elliott set his fork down and exhaled slowly.

What did it matter, in the end, if Odette's homage to Henry was biased? What did it matter if it was an act of love instead of truth?

"We'd want a say in what goes into it," Elliott said. "Into how it's presented."

Odette nodded. "You'd get the final say. You've got my fucking word on that."

Elliott nodded.

"I think we should do it," Marianne said. "Dad would love it."

Abby smiled at her. "I think *you* should do it. You and Elliott."

"Mom?" Elliott asked.

"Greta has school." Abby shrugged. "Someone needs to stay with her. Putting together an exhibit like that could take a while, isn't that right, Odette?"

Odette nodded.

"So you'd be hiring my kids too? Just like my painting?"

Odette snorted. "I can give 'em a room above the gallery, a *per diem*, and a fuck of a good reference that calls them my assistants. That's all the blood you'll get out of this stone, Abby. I'm not a fucking charity."

It was clearly a lie. Elliott couldn't think of any other reason Odette was here, except to offer them some help in her own brusque way. This wasn't just for Henry. This was for Abby and her children as well.

Elliott wondered if he and Marianne could really do it. If they were really in the right emotional state to sift through their dad's things and pick out those pieces that made a picture of him.

He caught Marianne's gaze, and she flashed him a brilliant smile.

Elliott returned it cautiously.

What would his own retrospective look like? Would it be an eclectic mix of bright colors and beautiful, random things? Would anyone sweep a net through the detritus of Elliott's life and pick out enough pieces to make something approaching a whole? What would people think if they walked into a space and saw Elliott Dashwood's life on display?

Elliott couldn't help but imagine a quiet room full of blank canvases and empty staring faces.

***

Before she left, Odette spent an evening at the Boathouse, drinking wine on the verandah and glaring at the lake as though it had personally offended her.

"It's so picturesque I want to vomit," she announced.

Paula looked startled. "We've had interest from investors about building a resort!"

Odette cocked an eyebrow.

"The Ferrars Corporation," Paula said. "Have you heard of them?"

"Honey, I'm not saying it's not pretty," Odette said firmly. "I'm just saying it's not for me."

Elliott steered Paula away, deposited her in Marianne's company, and fetched a fresh glass of wine for Odette. When he returned to her side, he spotted Greta and Poppy and Violet sitting down by the lakeshore, their faces illuminated by the glow of their phones.

John was late to arrive home, and when he finally joined them, he was accompanied by Colonel Brandon. She looked as uncomfortable as always, holding herself stiffly. She waved away John's offer of a drink.

"No," she said. "Not with my meds."

"Ah," John said. "And how is the yoga going?"

"Um. Slowly." Her expression grew even more discomforted, and Elliott thought of the DVD shards rattling around in the case.

John patted her shoulder awkwardly. "Well, listen, I've got a friend who's recommended me a yogi who specializes in rehab. I don't think there are any DVDs, but I believe the classes are online."

Colonel Brandon pursed her mouth into a thin line, then sighed. "I'll give it a try."

Elliott moved away, not wanting to eavesdrop.

John fired up the grill, and within the hour everyone was sitting around the table eating tofu burgers.

"Tastes just like steak, doesn't it?" John beamed.

"No," Colonel Brandon said. "It really doesn't."

John's laughter boomed out into the cool evening air.

The talk eventually turned to Henry's exhibit.

"Oh, you'll be in New York?" Colonel Brandon asked Marianne.

"My, um, my daughter lives there. I fly out to see her every few months."

"You have a daughter?" Marianne asked.

A sudden silence seemed to settle over the table, and Elliott caught the glance that passed between John and Paula.

"My adopted daughter." Colonel Brandon's tone was brusque. "Eliza. She goes to Hofstra."

"Another soda water?" Paula asked brightly, nudging the bottle toward Colonel Brandon.

Marianne leaned around Paula to continue the conversation. "If you're in New York when the exhibit's on, you'll have to come and see it. We'd love to have some people there who aren't just the usual arrogant assholes who go to these things."

"Hey!" Odette snorted. "Those are my valued clients you're talking about."

"Oh, please," Marianne said. "*You* call them arrogant assholes."

"That's true." Odette laughed. "I sell art to people who don't even look at it. They buy it because it's an investment, not because it speaks to them. And then they go and hang it on a wall in their house, where they also keep furniture they're too afraid to sit on and bottles of wine they can never open. These people are so fixated on things appreciating in value that they never let themselves experience them. What's the point of a vase you're never going to put flowers in, or a Queen Anne chair you can't just plant your ass on?"

Elliott thought of Norland Park. He thought of the old piano stool that Henry had used as a table. He thought of the chipped china they used at every meal, and of teacups with delicate floral patterns that were used to mix paints. He thought of the old silver coffee pot that Abby had used as a watering can for her herb garden. In another branch of the Family those things might have been locked up in glass-fronted cabinets, to be looked at and admired but never touched. Of course Cynthia and Aldous and Great Uncle Montgomery had been horrified, like a visit to Norland Park had been a front row seat to the Vandals' sacking of Rome.

"Life is for living, Elliott," Henry had said. *"Every part of it."*

And eggshell china was for mixing paints in.

He felt the familiar ache of his grief, and drew a slow, deep breath as he looked out over the lake.

Miss you, Dad.

***

Odette was staying at the three-star motel on the outskirts of town. There was a cell phone repair shop on one side of the hotel, and a landscaping supplies place on the other. Elliott was willing to bet Odette had never stayed somewhere where the rooms opened directly into the parking lot before.

"You will come, won't you?" she asked him as they pulled in.

"To New York?" Elliott chewed his bottom lip for a moment. "I mean, yeah, Mom seems to really like the idea."

"She does. She knows I won't fuck Henry's legacy over. But I want you onboard with this, Elliott. I want this to be something you want to do for yourself, not just for Abby or Marianne."

Elliott glanced at her, and then away.

"Yes, you are that transparent." Odette snorted. "You always were a good kid, Elliott. Do you remember when I came out to visit your guys years ago and your parents took us to that awful beach for a picnic?"

Elliott laughed. Everything without climate control was awful to Odette. "Yeah."

"You must have been ten or eleven. And it started to rain, and Henry said, 'Oh! Did Elliott bring the umbrellas?' Ten years old and you were the fucking parent."

"I remember that," Elliott said, staring out the windshield at the deserted parking lot.

"Meanwhile, Marianne was lying on her stomach in the shallows, splashing around like a crazy thing." Odette huffed out a quiet laugh. "Because it was already raining and she couldn't get more wet."

"She had a point," Elliott said softly. He turned his head to look at Odette.

"That Brandon woman." Odette raised her eyebrows. "She has a very obvious and painful crush on your sister."

Elliott smiled slightly. "Everyone who meets her has a very obvious and painful crush on Marianne."

"And what about you? Who in the world has a crush on Elliott?"

Elliott hesitated for a moment, shoving down a flash of unnamable emotion at the thought of Ned, and then shrugged. "Nobody I know of."

Odette raised her eyebrows. "There's more to that story, isn't there?" She patted him on the arm. "Never mind. Come to New York, and I'll find you someone to take your mind off it."

"I'll come to New York," Elliott said, "but not because I need you to find me a boyfriend."

"Who was talking about a boyfriend? I was talking about getting you laid, Elliott, not married."

"I'm good, thanks," Elliott said wryly. "In fact, I'll only come to New York if you promise not to pimp me out."

"Sweetheart." Odette tilted her head to look at him on an angle. "With that pretty face, you'd make us both a fortune."

Elliott snorted. "Get out of the car, Odette, or I'll drive you back into town."

Odette opened the door, laughing as she stepped outside. "See you in New York, sweetheart!"

"Yeah," Elliott said. "See you there."

She waved at him in the rearview as he drove out of the motel parking lot and turned back toward Barton Lake.

CHAPTER 13

The Blue Leaf Gallery was located on Green Street, SoHo, between Prince and Spring Streets, in a building with a cast iron exterior typical of the neighborhood. It had been there in one form or another since the 1960s. Odette had taken over in the early nineties, and had resisted moving to Chelsea like a wave of other galleries had. Elliott had first visited as a child, his patience rewarded with a promise of going to the nearest bookstore once Henry and Odette had finished talking business. To amuse himself in the meantime, Elliott had looked at all the paintings and artworks in the gallery and, when that no longer held his attention, had attempted to count the bricks in the whitewashed walls.

He felt a sense of something a little like homecoming as he pushed open the door and was greeted with a burst of warm air that overwhelmed the chill in the air outside. Fall in New York; Elliott had forgotten how stealthily sharp the air could be. He stepped inside, his backpack on his shoulder, with Marianne following.

The gallery was much like Elliott remembered. White walls, spotlights, paintings and sculptures. It was a familiar space, even though all the art was new since Elliott had been here last, and comforting.

"Hello!" A young man, slim-hipped and platinum blond, stepped briskly toward them with a bright smile on his face. He was wearing skinny jeans so dark they looked almost black, boots with Cuban heels, and a dress shirt that clung to the planes of his torso. "Can I help you? Oh! Wait! Are you Elliott and Marianne?"

"Hi." Elliott extended his hand. "That's us."

The young man's smile vanished abruptly. "Omigosh! You were supposed to send Odette your arrival time so I could arrange a car!"

"It was fine," Elliott said. "We got the bus to Jackson Heights, and then the subway."

The young man pressed his hand to his chest. "Odette is going to flay me alive!" He shuddered, but then his smile was back. "I'm Lucien, by the way, Odette's assistant. I'm so glad to meet you. We just got the last box of your father's papers in last week, but we didn't open anything yet. Odette thought it was best to wait for you."

Elliott exhaled. "Oh, okay."

Lucien studied him closely. "Or . . . or I could go through them first if it's something you're not ready to do?"

Elliott felt a rush of gratitude. He looked to Marianne.

"That's so sweet," she said, "but Elliott and I want to do it."

"Okay," Lucien said. "Totally understandable. Everything's upstairs for you to get started on whenever you like." His eyes widened. "Oh, wow, where are my manners? Obviously first you need to freshen up, and then we're going to go to lunch. How does that sound?"

"Lunch?" Marianne asked hopefully.

"Odette's uptown at a meeting," Lucien dug into the pocket of his skinny jeans and tugged out a card. "But look who has the company credit card! And, I mean, I could take you to a restaurant, but meanwhile the deli on the next block has the most a-*maz*-ing sandwiches. Seriously, the *best*. I mean, I know you're living in California now, but you still do carbs, right?"

"Oh, we still do carbs," Marianne assured him. "All the carbs."

Lucien leaned in toward her, eyes wide, as though he was about to impart a great secret. "We are going to be *best* friends!"

Marianne laughed, delighted.

"But first let's get you upstairs." Lucien crossed over to his desk—an antique piece still very much in use—opened the drawer, then returned with a set of keys. "Okay, so this one's for the gallery, and this one's for the apartment. I'll show you how to work the alarm later, in case you're coming and going after hours."

He led them toward the old service elevator behind the desk, and pulled the cage open.

The gallery itself was two floors. Odette also owned a loft apartment on the third floor, which she accessed via the service elevator, and a smaller apartment beside that which she often rented to her artists in residence. Odette had a long history of supporting the artists who supported her.

As the rattling elevator took them upward, Lucien continued to talk. "So there's a bodega two blocks south of here that's open pretty much around the clock. We can pick you up some groceries after lunch, or you can just eat out if you want." He patted his flat abdomen. "I know where all the best food trucks are. Look at what they've done to me!"

"You're completely gorgeous," Marianne said earnestly.

Lucien laughed, color rising in his cheeks. "I wasn't fishing, I promise, but you are so sweet!"

The elevator stopped on the third floor, and Lucien opened the cage. "You guys have stayed here before, right?"

"Actually, no," Elliott said. The elevator opened onto a small foyer with two doors that led off it. Elliott nodded toward the door on the right. "We've been to Odette's place before, but we've never stayed."

"Oh." Lucien flicked through the keys. "Well, it's a studio apartment, sorry, which means one of you has the couch."

"That would be me," Marianne said.

Oh, thank God. Elliott was tired of sleeping on a couch.

Marianne threw him a knowing look as Lucien opened the door and they followed him inside. The apartment was small, and furnished sparsely but with great care. The furniture and fixtures were sleek and modern, but Elliott liked that the bones of the place were old. Uneven brickwork, an arch that might have been open once but was now a wall, and high ceilings.

Lucien passed the keys to Marianne. "Okay, so I'll see you downstairs when you're ready for lunch!"

Elliott poked around the apartment. He set his backpack down on the bed, and helped Marianne investigate how easy it would be to fold out the couch. Then he checked the mini fridge in the corner, and the small bathroom.

"God," Marianne said from the main room. "Can you believe we came all this way and Jack's not even here?"

Elliott opened and closed the small vanity under the sink. He hummed sympathetically. To say that Marianne had been looking forward to seeing Jack again was an understatement, but the timing hadn't worked out. Jack was out of town, doing something with some law firm. Some internship or something. Marianne had been vague on the details.

"Maybe I could go visit him in Chicago," she said. "Surprise him one weekend."

"Maybe." Elliott stepped outside again. "Do you want the first sh—"

"Yes!" Marianne exclaimed, rushing past him and slamming the bathroom door shut. "Lucien seems nice!" she called from behind the door.

"Uh huh." Elliott crossed over to the window and tugged it open. The air outside was cool, and Elliott leaned out the window. There was a rickety-looking fire escape clinging to the side of the building. Cars inched down the street, and pedestrians darted between them. Across the street, in a building that mirrored this one, a woman was sitting on the fire escape with a cigarette in one hand and a phone in the other.

There was something soothing about the rhythm of a city. Something comforting in the vastness of it. The anonymity. Nobody here knew he was a Dashwood. Nobody here cared. In Barton Lake, Elliott could see a shift when people looked at him like he was something they couldn't puzzle out: A *Dashwood*? Waiting tables?

Elliott didn't care that he was waiting tables. He just didn't want to have to explain why he was doing it. Not when the story started with him holding Henry's hand. Not when it started with a broken promise.

"John, promise me that you'll look after your brother and your sisters."

Elliott didn't want to pick that scab open every day.

Anonymity felt good.

He went and sat on the bed and waited for Marianne to finish in the shower. He left the window open, so that the sounds of the city drifted inside.

***

Lucien was absolutely right about the deli. The sandwiches were amazing. Elliott had already eaten most of his by the time they walked back to the gallery.

"So, you guys are going to be here for a few weeks at least, right?" Lucien asked, holding the door of the gallery open for them. "Because we have got to go out at least once."

"Elliott is allergic to fun," Marianne said with a sly smile, elbowing him in the ribs. "But yes, that's definitely a thing we have to do."

"I hate clubbing," Elliott said.

"Have you ever *been* clubbing?" Marianne asked him.

"No. But I hate crowds, and loud music, and staying up too late."

Marianne rolled her eyes. "Lucien, have you met Elliott? He's a middle-aged man trapped in this twink's body."

Lucien laughed, his perfect teeth gleaming. "Oh! No, Elliott, really, you'll like the place I've got in mind. It's a small place, and they do live music and poetry slams, and it's full of hipsters and scene kids, plus there's an awesome taqueria right next door. And I promise to have you home before you turn into a pumpkin."

"Maybe," Elliott said warily. "I don't know if it's really my sort of thing."

"Elliott!" Marianne wormed into the space under his arm and hugged him. "Please!"

Marianne's tone was light and teasing, but there was real concern in her gaze. She worried about him, Elliott knew. She worried that looking after their dad during his illness, and now the rest of them, had somehow stolen something from him. Some intangible experience of youth that he should feel cheated about, but he didn't. He loved his family. Whatever sacrifices he'd made . . . they weren't *obligations*. They weren't a weight. Maybe they would have been to Marianne, but not to Elliott.

They ate their lunch at Lucien's desk while he talked about the place he wanted to take them to, and a few other things in the neighborhood they might want to do. Then he talked about the project.

"So, we got a bunch of boxes of your father's things last week," he said with a tiny grimace that might have been an acknowledgement of their grief or, just as likely, an acknowledgement of the hell they must have gone through dealing with the Family. Elliott was half-surprised they hadn't just tossed everything in the trash. "There are a lot of papers in there, and photographs, and diaries. That sort of thing.

What Odette wants you guys to do is go through and find the stuff that will show people where Henry got his inspiration from."

"Pot, mostly," Marianne said.

"You joke," Lucien said, "but I think I saw a roach clip in there somewhere."

"Honestly, that's just as likely to be Mom's." Marianne finished her sandwich and stretched. "Okay, I'm ready to take a look. Elliott?"

"Sure," Elliott said, forcing his uncertainty away. "Let's get started."

***

The second floor of the gallery was closed to the public. It was a wide, open area with polished floorboards, white brick walls, and empty hooks. There was a stack of at least eight large boxes in the middle of the floor.

"I'm told this is basically everything from your father's studio that wasn't related to finances and stuff." Lucien trailed his fingers along the top of one box. "Odette hasn't talked much about what happened, but I'm really sorry you never got the chance to do this the proper way."

"There's a proper way?" Elliott asked quietly.

Lucien smiled slightly. "I don't know. Maybe?"

Marianne ripped the tape off the first box; a dry, rasping sound. She opened the box and reached inside. "Oh," she said, surprised, withdrawing an item. "This is going to be messy."

She wasn't talking about the dust.

She turned and showed Elliott what she'd taken out of the box. A framed photograph. Elliott with a gap-toothed smile. Marianne beaming beside him, her pigtails lopsided. Greta, wearing only a diaper, standing between them, her mouth open and most of her spitty fist jammed inside.

"Oh." A sudden wave of grief and homesickness hit Elliott.

Lucien put a hand on his shoulder and squeezed. "You know what? I'm going to leave you guys to it. But I'll be right downstairs if you need anything. Kleenex. Chocolate. Hard liquor."

Elliott smiled despite himself. "Thanks."

Lucien left them to it, and Elliott and Marianne ripped open the other boxes. There was no order to it. There was no plan. They dug in. Pulled out papers and diaries. Some they flicked through. Others they set aside for later. There were a few more photographs, portfolios of sketches, newspaper clippings that had obviously caught Henry's eye at one time. There were finger paintings and crayon drawings that they'd made for him. Thumbprint people he'd shown them how to create. Elliott wondered what those would look like next to Henry's actual works. He wondered if people would frown when they saw them, and ask themselves what they were doing in an exhibit, or if they would think of their own families and smile.

"This is going to be harder than I thought," Marianne said, pulling out a photo album. "This wasn't in Dad's study, was it?"

Elliott took the album from her, running his fingers over the cover. He opened it. "It's their wedding album."

Henry and Abby smiled out from the pages.

A courthouse wedding. A few friends. No Family. Odette was there, looking like she hadn't aged a day. She hadn't, probably, though sheer force of will. There were a few other people Elliott recognized. Friends of their parents. Strange, but he'd never thought whose friends. He'd never wondered if his father had brought any of them over from his old life. Maybe he had, or maybe they'd all shunned him. Told him he was stupid to choose the woman over the money. Because that's what it had been, and not just in the end. The Family had never tolerated Henry's choice; they'd packed him off to Massachusetts so they could ignore it. They'd never accepted it, and they'd never accepted Abby, Elliott, Marianne, or Greta.

Sins of the father.

Damned in perpetuity.

Something like that.

It hadn't seemed strange to Elliott, growing up. It was just the way things were. But now, he tried to think of any reason he'd shun Marianne like that, or Greta. He couldn't think of one.

"I think I'm glad they didn't like us," he said, touching the thin sheet of plastic that covered his father's smiling face. "Can you imagine what assholes we would have turned out to be if they had?"

"God," Marianne said, eyes wide. "*Such* assholes." She snatched the album back. "But with *impeccable* table manners!"

Elliott looked at the album. "I think that was in their bedroom closet, wasn't it?"

"Was it?" Marianne asked, her brow creased.

"I think so." Elliott warmed with affection for John, who must have put everything together. The album easily could have ended up in a trash heap somewhere, and probably would have if anyone else in the Family had been in change. This way, even if they didn't need it for the exhibit, they could take it home to Abby.

He should text John. Thank him.

They continued to sort through the boxes.

"What is Odette aiming for, do you think?" Marianne asked at one point, her brow furrowed. "I mean, who are we supposed to be looking for in here? Henry Dashwood the artist, or Dad?"

"I don't know. I guess maybe the point where they intersect?"

It was hard.

"I wish Mom was here," Marianne said quietly when she pulled one of Henry's paint-stained palettes from a box. The paint was dried in globs on the surface of the palette, like the ridges and dips on a contour map.

"Yeah." Elliott reached for the palette and bent his neck to see if he could catch the scent of the paint still. He wondered if the paints on it were from Henry's last project, or if this was the palette Elliott had used that day he and Ned had . . .

Warmth rose in him, and he felt himself flush.

Jerked each other off frantically against a canvas?

There was no way to say that without it sounding filthy. Which it had been, in all the best ways. Elliott had been picking paint out of his hair half the way to California.

Still, he regretted it as well, and not just because of the way things had worked out—or hadn't—with Ned. Mostly he regretted how it had led to their very hasty departure from Norland Park. He wished they'd had longer to pack. If Abby hadn't been fuming with righteous indignation, no way in hell would she have forgotten her wedding album. And okay, she'd get that back now, at least, but what about Greta's favorite t-shirt? What about the little things they hadn't even missed yet?

Marianne flipped through a sketchbook. "I think that whole thing about Mom having to stay in California because of Greta's school was bullshit." She met Elliott's gaze. "Since when has Mom cared about stuff like school? Also, she could have left Greta with John and Paula. I think she just didn't want to come."

"I think you're right," Elliott said. "I think that she wants us to do this because she knew she couldn't. I don't know if she's even really accepted it yet, you know?"

All that positive thinking, all that healthy eating and meditation and yoga, and none of it had made a difference.

"Elliott," Henry had said toward the end, *"you'll watch out for your mom, won't you? She's going to take this hard, I think."*

As though Elliott somehow wouldn't? Except he knew what his dad meant. His dad's illness hadn't fundamentally changed Elliott's worldview. His death hadn't. Abby, though... Abby hadn't been ready because she hadn't really believed it would happen.

"We'll be okay though," Elliott said quietly. "You and me, we can do this, Mar."

"Yeah." Marianne sniffed and wiped her eyes on the cuff of her sleeve. "It's gonna be messy though."

"Yeah," Elliott murmured. "It is."

***

Odette appeared back at the gallery just before six with two pizzas and a six-pack of imported beer. Lucien doled out napkins, and they sat around on the floor, surrounded by the detritus of Henry's life, and ate.

"The paintings from Norland Park are in storage," Odette said. "Now I want to sell them all. More sales for me is more money for you and your mom, so yes, let's be fucking mercenary about this. That's why I want you kids here. I can sell paintings to people, but you're the only one who can sell your father."

Marianne nodded.

Elliott's gaze fell on the wedding album. "Thank you. For doing this. For getting John to send Dad's things."

"Oh, that wasn't me. John finds me 'abrasive and unpleasant.'" Air quotes. Odette huffed. "He barely wanted to deal with me long enough to get the paintings sorted out. It was Lucien who performed this little miracle."

Elliott looked at Lucien, eyebrows raised.

"I am neither abrasive nor unpleasant," Lucien said brightly.

Odette huffed and reached for a slice of pizza.

They talked a little while they ate, their memories of Henry and Norland Park tumbling out here and there. Odette told them about the first time she'd met him, about her assumption that someone with the surname Dashwood might be a dilettante at best and nothing but an over-inflated ego at worst. And her surprise when she'd discovered a real artist instead.

"He started painting so late," she said, picking an olive off her slice and flicking it back into the box. "If he hadn't spent the first thirty years of his life being forced into the box built by the rest of his goddamn family, he could have been phenomenal."

Elliott glanced over at the boxes and wondered if that was true. If his dad could have been great if only he'd gone to art school instead of business school. If only he'd picked up a paintbrush before he'd met Abby. If only he'd had the time.

When the pizza and beer were finished, Odette and Marianne gathered up the trash and headed downstairs with it.

Elliott found his gaze drawn to the boxes again. He felt Lucien watching him quietly, and pulled his gaze away again. "Thank you. For doing this. For having to deal with them."

"I happened to have an in," Lucien said, flushing. "Okay, promise you won't tell anyone? It's sort of a secret."

"Okay," Elliott said.

"John's wife," Lucien said. "Francesca. I'm engaged to her brother."

Elliott froze. "Her brother?"

Lucien smiled. "I'm engaged to Ned. Ned Ferrars. I have been for three years now."

"To Ned?" A cold, dark pressure expanded in Elliott's chest. "You're engaged to Ned?"

"Oh God, I *know*!" Lucien laughed. "The whole family's so awful, but Ned's not like them, I promise! He's really kind and wonderful and a total cinnamon roll, really."

Elliott forced himself to smile.

Forced himself not to react.

Forced himself to breathe as he listened to Lucien explain how Ned Ferrars was the sweetest guy he'd ever met.

CHAPTER 14

"Elliott, are you okay?" Marianne asked as they entered the apartment.

"Fine," Elliott said numbly.

It didn't matter.

Marianne threw him a worried look.

It didn't matter. Ned hadn't promised anything. It was just a hook up. Hadn't Elliott said that all along? It didn't matter. This sense of . . . of whatever the hell it was, was misplaced. It was all his stupid hope, crushed, but that burden was Elliott's alone. Elliott had built that hope up out of nothing, and it was his own fault because Ned hadn't promised anything.

Marianne raised her eyebrows. "Was it the pizza?"

Elliott shrugged. He knew better than to blame his nausea on the pizza and beer. And even while he forced a smile, a part of him marveled at how Marianne couldn't tell. How was he not transparent as glass in this moment? But that was one thing Elliott had always been good at, wasn't it? Repressing his feelings.

"Don't you ever get angry?"

Elliott almost smiled at the memory, something tight and bitter tugging in his chest.

Ned hadn't promised anything.

There had been nothing to promise.

Just a series of dumb mistakes that had culminated in one frantic, messy moment up against a wet canvas. Just forced proximity. Just Elliott being so unanchored in those days, so confused and numb and in shock still that he'd done something he normally wouldn't. With a guy who had a fiancé, apparently, but fuck that. That wasn't Elliott's fault.

Lucien was so friendly and welcoming that Elliott hated himself right now, but it wasn't his fault. Ned could have told him. *Should* have told him. Well, Ned had them both fooled, didn't he? Elliott and Lucien. Turned out he was just another rich, entitled asshole who thought he could do what he wanted.

If Ned were here now, Elliott would show him just how angry he could get.

Maybe.

Fuck. Who was he kidding? Of course he wouldn't. He'd be too fucking humiliated to even look at him.

"Do you think you're coming down with something?" Marianne was still wearing her worried frown.

Elliott drew a deep breath and crossed over to the bed, then sat down heavily and rubbed his hands over his face. "Fuck."

Marianne sat down beside him and rubbed his back in small circles, like their mom did when they were sick. "Elliott?"

"It—" Elliott snorted, and sat up. "Sorry. I'm just tired, I think. And seeing Dad's stuff . . ."

He felt a stab of guilt for using that as an excuse when Marianne's eyes widened. "I know. God, I *know*."

Elliott forced a smile. "A shower will make me feel a lot better."

"Okay." Marianne's worry evaporated when her phone chimed, and she tugged it out of her pocket. A smile lit up her face when she looked at the screen.

Jack.

Elliott escaped to the sanctuary of the bathroom, away from Marianne's misplaced sympathy and, worse, her happiness. Elliott knew he wouldn't be able to listen to her prattle on about Jack without it turning into something bitter and jealous inside him, and he didn't want to be that asshole.

God. It was . . . it *hurt*. It hurt because he'd liked Ned, and he'd thought Ned liked him too, but it turned out that Elliott was just a fool.

It was only under the hot spray of the shower that the strange truth occurred to him: it hadn't been John who'd put the photo album in with Henry's other belongings. It had been Ned.

Somehow the kindness of his gesture just made it hurt more.

***

His first decent bed in weeks, and Elliott couldn't sleep. He lay awake and listened to Marianne breathe, and watched the play of light and shadow on the ceiling. He hated how Ned Ferrars was so hard to exorcise. Elliott should have been able to do it back in Barton Lake, when Ned had been so cool toward him. Had that been guilt? Elliott hoped so.

"Don't you ever get angry?" Ned had asked him back at Norland Park.

Yeah. Yeah, Elliott got angry sometimes. Turned out that cheating assholes got him angry, particularly when they'd made him an unknowing accomplice in their shitty behavior. He was tempted to grab his phone and send Ned a text. Tell him exactly how angry he was. Except that was a dumb idea. The dumbest. Because then Ned would know exactly how much he was hurt, and Ned didn't deserve to know he had that power over Elliott.

It hurt.

It hurt because Ned back at Norland Park had seemed so kind, so genuine. He hadn't looked at Elliott like he was nothing, like he was an inconvenience. He'd treated Elliott and his grief with respect, or so Elliott had thought. He'd given Elliott a moment of respite, a brief sanctuary from the utter shit storm that was John and Francesca and the rest of them. Elliott had been so tired of running interference between Abby and the girls and the Family. He hadn't had to do that with Ned. He hadn't had to be on his guard.

Or so he'd thought.

It didn't matter.

What had he thought, anyway? That there was something there? That somehow there was a *future* in it? With Francesca's brother? People from families like that, they didn't welcome people like Elliott. Elliott *knew* that. He'd known that his entire life. The Ferrars family was no different. And nothing that had happened at Norland Park between him and Ned had been a solid enough foundation to build his stupid hopes on anyway.

This wasn't heartbreak.

This was the humiliating realization that he'd been stupid, and Elliott could deal with that. He'd dealt with worse, hadn't he?

He thought of his dad's things, spread out all over the gallery floor downstairs.

He'd dealt with a lot worse.

***

The Naked Blue Lady arrived in New York a week into Elliott and Marianne's stay, and Elliott watched anxiously as she was unloaded from the truck and carried inside in layers and layers of protective wrap. Elliott had already seen the mock ups of the postcards and magnets Odette had ordered. No tote bags, thankfully. Odette had settled on a less confronting piece for those: a landscape that was unlikely to get anyone banned from Whole Foods.

Elliott and Marianne were slowly coming to grips with the contents of the boxes from Norland Park. It felt a little like trying to assemble a jigsaw puzzle with no idea of what they even wanted the final picture to look like. The entire process was emotionally draining. They both took frequent breaks to laugh, or to cry, or to work off their frustration with a walk to the deli and back to get emergency junk food.

Lucien was a constant visitor to the second floor. Sometimes it was to let them know he had to head out for a moment and was locking up. Sometimes it was to remind them to take a break for lunch. Sometimes it was just to chat. He was friendly, and warm, and Elliott hated how guilty that made him feel. He hadn't known, but that was no consolation.

Lucien was excited to take them to the slam poetry place he loved, and was disappointed when Elliott feigned a headache. Marianne went instead, and was back hours later, trying to sneak quietly into the apartment in the darkness, and swearing when she stubbed her toe on the couch.

"How was it?" Elliott asked, reaching out to turn the bedside lamp on.

Marianne shrugged her coat off, and then tugged her knit cap off. She leaned against the couch. "It was really good. You would have liked it, I think."

Yeah, he really would have liked sitting across from the guy whose fiancé he'd cheated with.

Marianne looked at him. "You are allowed to have fun sometimes you know, Elliott?"

"I know, Mar. I'm just tired."

Guilty, more like.

It wasn't just guilt, though. There was something else there too, something that Elliott didn't want to think about too closely. It tasted a little like jealousy, and he hated it. He didn't want to get into another conversation with Lucien about Ned. He didn't want to hear about how wonderful Ned was, how happy he made Lucien. Not when he'd once cultivated those same stupid hopes. Cultivated them out of thin air, as it turned out, but it didn't make them any less painful to crush.

Elliott wished his dad were here to give his perspective. His dad had been a cheater too, once upon a time. Not that Henry and Abby had framed their story like that. No. Theirs was a story of fate, of love as unstoppable as a force of nature. Theirs was a story that was so vast, so all-encompassing that there wasn't any room for the people left behind. For the first Mrs. Dashwood. For John.

Had Henry ever regretted that?

Elliott wished he'd had the courage to ask.

***

Over the next few days, the exhibit slowly took shape around them. Marianne divided her time between working through Henry's things and flirting with Jack via text. Elliott didn't have a happy distraction like she did. He became immersed in his dad's things, picking through them like he was some sort of archaeologist trying to piece together an entire person from only the bones that remained. He tried to ignore the strange disconnect he felt now between the man whose image he was creating for the consumption of strangers, the father he'd loved, and the man who'd caused so much hurt to others in his pursuit of love.

Growing up, John had sometimes come to visit when he was on vacation from his fancy school. Elliott could remember waiting for him, feeling that strange mix of nervousness and guilt. Even at a young age he'd been aware that his relationship with his dad was very different from John's. That he and John were brothers, but they could never be friends. The age gap was bad enough. The rest was insurmountable. At best John felt like some sort of distant cousin who turned up occasionally, looked unhappy to be there, and then left again.

There was one night . . .

Elliott must have been eight or nine. Henry had been chasing them around, roaring like a dinosaur to make a toddling Greta screech with delight. He'd been wearing his paint-splattered clothes, with a brush tucked carelessly behind one ear. His fingers were claws, and he'd stalked them through the house. Even Elliott had been breathless with laughter.

And then some movement had caught his eye and he'd turned and seen John watching from the doorway. He was way too old for stupid games by then—Elliott was probably way too old as well—but there'd been such an expression of longing on his face that it had brought Elliott up short. And then John had walked away.

The game hadn't been fun after that.

Elliott had excused himself, unable to feel happy about playing if John couldn't. And, even if he didn't properly understand it at that age, he knew one thing for certain: John couldn't.

"John," Henry had said on his deathbed. *"John, promise me that you'll look after your brother and your sisters."*

What a cruel thing that was to ask.

What a cruel thing love could be, when it was stripped back to its bones.

***

There was a painting on the bottom floor of the gallery that Elliott was drawn to. A lonely figure looking away. A green background that suggested chaos, a maelstrom. Struggle. Elliott's chest tightened when he looked at it. He didn't know who it represented to him. Himself maybe. Maybe his dad. Maybe nobody. Maybe everybody.

When he closed his eyes at night and tried to sleep, he thought of the figure in the painting standing there silently. Enduring.

He ached.

***

Abigail in Lamplight dominated the room. Her pose was provocative, but her smile was shy. Elliott had built up a lifetime of immunity to the painting, and he couldn't help letting out a small laugh when Lucien gasped.

"Oh, wow. That's, um, so that's your mom, and that's your mom's . . ." He cleared his throat. "It's so much bigger than I thought it would be."

Elliott looked at him, eyebrows raised.

"The painting!" Lucien exclaimed, a flush climbing up his throat and staining his cheeks red. "The entirety of the painting, not . . ." He gestured vaguely. "Oh, Jesus. Kill me now, please."

Elliott laughed again. "You should have seen the looks I got when I brought kids home for sleepovers and this was one of the first things they saw in the house. I had a friend from eighth grade who couldn't speak to me again until about a week before we graduated senior year."

"Eighth grade is a confusing time," Lucien said, rubbing the back of his neck. "Nobody wants to think about what their friends' parents have under their clothes in eighth grade."

"Right," Elliott said. "That's more of a ninth grade phenomenon."

"Damn straight." Lucien laughed. "My friend Jamon's dad? Freeballed it under his sweatpants and was at least ninety-five percent responsible for the fact that I figured out I was gay. Total DILF."

Elliot laughed too. "I don't think I ever had a revelation. I think I always knew. I didn't grow up in the sort of house where the assumption was that any of us were straight, you know? It was never the default. Mom and Dad had a lot of queer friends."

Elliott's otherness had nothing to do with his sexuality. He sometimes felt like he was the kid born in the circus who dreamed of running away to be an accountant.

"That's very cool," Lucien said, his smile softening.

Elliott stared at *Abigail in Lamplight* and then gazed around the gallery. His dad's diaries were here now, on display under glass. His brushes were. Some family photographs. Some sketches. Pictures of Norland Park. Ephemera. Detritus. "How . . . how do I show them that? The people who are going to come here? How do I show them what sort of man my dad was, when sometimes I don't even know myself?"

Lucien met his gaze.

"I mean, where are his meds? Where are the tubes and shit he had coming out of him in the hospital?" Elliott's eyes stung and his throat felt suddenly raw. "Where are all those pills he had to swallow that none of us were allowed to touch because they were so fucking toxic?" He cleared his throat. "What about all those photographs of me and my sisters? He had them pinned up all around his studio, but there wasn't a single one of John. So who was he? How could he be such a great dad for us, and just walk away from John like that?"

"I don't know," Lucien said quietly. "I don't know that."

"He wasn't perfect," Elliott rasped.

"Nobody is."

"He left us with fucking *nothing*." The words were out before Elliott could stop them. It felt as though they'd come from nowhere, but maybe they'd been building up for months. Years, possibly, because from the second he got his diagnosis, Henry could have done something. *Should* have done something. Shouldn't have left them with no income and no home. Elliott pressed the heels of his hands against his eyes. "Jesus *fuck*."

"Hey." Lucien pulled him into a hug. His aftershave smelled like citrus. "*Hey.*"

"Shit." Elliott pulled away, keeping his gaze averted. "Sorry. I'm sorry."

"For what?" Lucien asked gently. "You have nothing to apologize for."

God. Poor Lucien didn't know the half of it.

Elliott swallowed and scrubbed his face with his hands. "For being a mess all over you, I guess."

"Elliott." The fond smile was evident in Lucien's tone. "I was messier last week when I thought I'd lost my metro card."

"God." Elliott sucked in a breath. "Sorry. I don't even know where that came from. We're fine, you know? Jesus." He rolled his shoulders. "There's a guy next to the deli who keeps all his worldly goods in a shopping cart, and I'm complaining about fucking *what*? Not living in a mansion anymore?"

"Elliott."

Elliott took a moment to lift his gaze, half afraid he'd see condemnation in Lucien's eyes. He didn't, though. He just saw that same warmth that was evident in everything Lucien did.

"You know, my nonna always used to yell at me if I didn't want my dinner. Didn't I know there were children starving in Africa?" He shrugged. "Fat lot of good her meatballs would have done them though, right?"

"I don't think it's the same thing."

"It's absolutely the same thing," Lucien said. "Don't argue with me."

Elliott smiled despite himself.

"Also, we should get meatballs. And beer. Mostly beer."

"Mostly beer," Elliott agreed.

"And we're going to drink it all," Lucien said, "and get as messy as we want, and you can yell at your dad all you like. Get it out of your system before you have to smile and play nice for the buyers."

"I don't really . . ." Except there was no good way to say *I don't want to be your friend, Lucien*, was there? And not for anything that Lucien had done, but because of Elliott's own guilt. He forced a smile instead. "Actually, that sounds really good."

Lucien slung an arm around Elliott's shoulders. "Let's do this thing."

***

Marianne found them a few hours later, sprawled together on the floor of the gallery in front of *Abigail in Lamplight*, Lucien listening avidly while Elliott recounted the time his dad marched down to his school to complain when Elliott failed Art in sixth grade.

"And not because he thought I had to follow in his footsteps or anything, or that the son of Henry Dashwood might actually suck at art," Elliott said. "I was terrible. We all knew I was terrible. But because he didn't think anyone should fail art. He didn't think it was possible, because art is about *expression*, and there's no wrong way to express yourself."

"I remember that."

Elliot squinted toward the doorway, and smiled when he saw Marianne standing there.

"That is so incredible." Lucien shuffled aside to make room for Marianne to sit down between them. "You should tell that story. To the art people."

"I'm so bad at art," Elliott said with a sigh.

Marianne reached for Elliott's beer and took a sip. "How much have you boys had to drink?"

"Just enough," Lucien said, beaming at her.

"Just enough," Elliott agreed, and slung an arm around her shoulders.

They sat there a while longer, until Marianne, breathless with excitement, dashed outside for some privacy to take a call from Jack. Lucien passed Elliott another beer, and they sat and drank some more, surrounded by Henry's art.

CHAPTER 15

The day of the opening of the Henry Dashwood Retrospective dawned clear and cool. Elliott lay in bed as long as he could, dozing as Marianne showered and dressed and then sat cross-legged on the couch and spent a while scrolling though something on her phone. She stopped sometimes, her teeth digging into her bottom lip, and then smiled.

Elliott was looking forward to the opening, while at the same time the thought of it made him nervous. He wanted it to go well. He thought he and Marianne had done the best they could—Odette certainly seemed happy with them—but from now on it was out of their hands. Hopefully there would be a decent crowd. Hopefully his dad's paintings would sell. It wasn't just paint on canvas. It wasn't even windows into Henry's vision. It was more solid than that. It was a college fund for Marianne and Greta. It was health insurance. It was maybe getting a place with more room.

This was Henry's last paycheck, and while a part of Elliott hated to think of it in such a cold way, fuck art, right? It was money they needed, and money everyone was here for. Most of the people at the gallery tonight wouldn't be looking at the paintings and trying to understand the mind of the man behind them. Most of them would be calculating what those swathes of color were worth now that the man who'd put them there was dead.

Marianne set her phone on the arm of the couch and then stood up. She crossed over to the small refrigerator and rattled around in it for a moment. Then she walked over to the bed, pushed Elliott's feet out of the way, and sat down and began to pick through the remains of last night's falafel salad.

Elliott yawned and stretched.

"You need to get out of bed at some point," Marianne told him.

"Mmm."

"Lucien wants to make sure we have clothes for tonight. Like, I think he's going to vet our outfits."

Elliott had packed the single pair of dress pants he wore as a waiter, and a button-down shirt. He had the feeling those would not pass muster with Lucien, who always managed to look like he'd stepped off a billboard or fallen out of the glossy pages of a fashion magazine.

"Ugh." Elliott sat up and shuffled closer to Marianne. He picked an olive out of the salad.

It would be over tomorrow, and then they could pack up their dad's things that weren't being used for the display, and sort out getting them shipped to California. He would miss New York. He would miss being unnoticed here. He would miss feeling like a tiny part of something larger. He wouldn't miss digging through his dad's past, though, and his own. The wound still felt too fresh to go picking at the scab. He thought it might feel like that for years yet.

He'd miss New York, but he wanted to see his mom and Greta again. It had barely been three weeks, but Greta's text messages were increasingly hostile, and he was worried she was lonely: Barton Lake was boring. Greta's new school was so ugly it made her want to stab her eyes out with a pen. A bird was building a nest in a tree in their narrow back yard, and it was loud, Elliott, *loud*.

Greta just needed to vent to someone who would let her complain the glass was half empty, and that person was never going to be Abby.

Abby's texts had been much more optimistic. She'd finished her first lot of bead bracelets and sold two of them in the shop already. At fifteen dollars each! As though all their money troubles were now behind them, and she was on track to becoming some sort of bead bracelet entrepreneur.

Yeah. It was time to go back to Barton Lake.

Marianne's predictions about Lucien were proved correct when Lucien knocked on their door just after ten. He came bearing bags full of clothes.

"Okay, Dashwoods," he announced. "Let's make you beautiful! I have a bunch of my clothes for you to try, Elliott, and I borrowed some dresses off my friend's sister for Marianne."

Elliott eyed the pair of pants that Lucien hauled out of one of the bags. They were so skinny they looked more like leggings. "I don't think those will fit me."

"Oh, please. Of course they will. We're the same build."

Lucien's optimism proved misplaced ten minutes later when Elliott was struggling to pull the zip up on the pants. Lucien stood behind him, gripping the waistband of the pants and trying to hitch him into them while Marianne sat on the bed, red faced with laughter.

"Stop!" Elliott exclaimed. "They don't fit! Even if we get them up, I'll crush my balls if I try to walk!"

"Just try and breathe in," Lucien instructed.

"Stop trying to castrate my brother with pants!" Marianne said, gasping for breath and reaching for her phone.

Elliott grabbed for her arm. "Do *not* film this!"

"Okay," Lucien said. "Okay, take them off. I've got another pair that will work. I had to buy them last year after some asshole opened a bakery next door to my building. They sell *cronuts*, for fuck's sake. I'm not made of steel." He grimaced. "Not anymore, at least."

Elliott peeled the pants off with some difficulty. The next pair that Lucien handed him went on a little more easily, and Elliott could actually do the fly up. They were definitely tighter than anything he usually wore though.

"Nice!" Lucien exclaimed. "Those pants do incredible things to your ass. Seriously, if I wasn't already taken . . ." He winked.

Elliott forced a smile, and didn't look at Marianne. He was terrified she'd ask about Lucien's boyfriend. "So what shirt goes with it?"

"Oh, I have shirts and jackets," Lucien said. "And you're going to look amazing. FYI, I also brought hair gel, because those scruffy locks of yours are just crying out for help. I mean, you can get away with a little bit of a Bohemian vibe given that you're the son of an artist, but I have to draw the line somewhere."

It took another half an hour before Lucien was satisfied with Elliott's wardrobe, and then he turned his attention to Marianne. Marianne chose a green floor-length dress with a beaded halter neck that made her look effortlessly beautiful.

"It's vintage," Lucien said approvingly. "Heather has this knack for finding incredible clothes at rummage sales and Goodwill. It's like her superpower. You look *amazing* in that."

Marianne spun in a circle, and the dress billowed out. Elliott was immediately jealous that she hadn't been zipped into something constrictive.

"You could both so easily get laid tonight," Lucien said. "Seriously. I mean, I'd do it, but . . ."

"You're taken," Marianne said with a smile.

"Also totally gay. But you're giving me some serious vibes in the pants area, Marianne."

She laughed. "That is the sweetest and also strangest compliment I've ever gotten."

"Now, I need you both to get out of those clothes and keep them unwrinkled until tonight. In the meantime, let's go and get some cronuts. They're incredible, seriously. Life-changing. You'll see Jesus."

"Sounds like a plan," Elliott said, although anything that got him out of the pants sounded pretty damn sweet. The cronuts were just an added bonus.

***

Elliott felt like an imposter as he moved around the gallery, a flute of champagne in his hand and a smile fixed on his face. Marianne, her arm looped through his, was a natural at stuff like this. Marianne was the sun. Wherever she moved, everything else fell into orbit around her. She was perfectly at ease talking with strangers, unafraid of saying the wrong thing or of being unable to speak at all. She smiled brightly at strangers and fell easily into conversation, talking animatedly about Henry Dashwood her father, Henry Dashwood the artist, and Henry Dashwood the man.

The gallery was full, but Elliott didn't know if that meant anyone was buying or not. Odette worked the room with flawless precision, with Lucien at her side. Elliott caught Lucien's eye once, and Lucien's mouth quirked in a smile and he winked, and in that moment Elliott didn't feel so out of his depth. It was all a charade, wasn't it? The art, the people, life itself. It made him feel a little more certain of himself.

"What can you tell me about this painting?" a gruff man asked at one point, and Elliott realized he'd somehow detached himself from Marianne.

He looked at the painting. Three abstract figures painted in shades of brown and yellow, silhouetted against a stark red background. It wasn't his dad's usual style. It was . . . if Elliott had to pick a word, he'd say it was uglier.

"I remember when he painted it," Elliott said. "He started it the day after he was told the treatment wasn't working." He swallowed. "I never saw him angry. I think he put his anger into this piece."

The man's expression softened.

"I think he was very angry that he wouldn't get to see how we turned out. He always hated to leave things unfinished."

Three figures, though. Not four. John wasn't one of Henry's unfinished pieces. Elliott wondered at what point his dad had made that decision. He wondered, if Henry had lived long enough, if he would have done it for all of them at some point. Decided they were complete. It was impossible to know.

Elliott left the man gazing thoughtfully at the painting and stepped away. He didn't know if he'd made a sale or not. He didn't know if that was even the point anymore. It seemed like more of an accomplishment just to make it through a simple exchange without crumbling, in all honesty. Elliott would take his victories where he could find them.

He shook his head at the waiter who offered him fresh champagne.

Elliott spoke to a few more people after that, and kept a careful eye on the level of champagne in his glass. He didn't want to get drunk. Odette snagged him for some photographs at some point, for both the gallery's website and for some critics doing pieces on the exhibition. Elliott found himself in conversation with one of the critics after their photo op, and he told her a little about his dad's determination to finish enough works to put on a final show.

"I met Henry a few times," the woman said. "He loved openings. I deal with a lot of egos in this business. Henry was never one of those."

"Thank you," Elliott said, the familiar ache expanding in his chest. "He loved art, and he always wanted everyone to love it as much as he did."

The woman gave him a sympathetic smile and brushed her hand along his forearm. She opened her mouth as though to speak, but then closed it again.

Maybe she had nothing to say. What was the appropriate thing to say to the person whose grief was laid out in the gallery around her? Pieces of it discreetly offered for sale. And downstairs, tote bags and magnets.

The woman squeezed his arm, and then moved on.

Elliott, feeling suddenly unanchored, went and found Marianne again.

***

Hours later, the caterers were leaving, and Odette was striding back and forth across the gallery floor in bare feet. Her stilettos lay abandoned in the middle of the room. She was jabbing at something on her tablet as she walked. Lucien was standing nearby, nodding along as she rattled names and numbers at him. Elliott didn't recognize the names, and he didn't know if the numbers were great or not.

"That's seven pieces sold already," Odette said. "Not too poor for an opening. And the exhibit's open for another month. I can shift the rest by then."

Elliott stooped down to pick up a discarded napkin, unsure what response was required.

Odette watched him knowingly. "It's good, Elliott. We did good."

Elliott balled the napkin up, relief settling over him.

Odette tucked her tablet under her arm. "Now I know that you're probably anxious to drag Marianne back to that godforsaken town in California, but Lucien here has managed the impossible and secured us reservations at Five for tomorrow night."

"At where?"

"It's a restaurant. At the moment, it's *the* restaurant." She raised her eyebrows, leaving the question unasked.

Elliott sighed.

Marianne bounced over to him, her eyes wide. "Oh, Elliott! Let's do it! Come on! I want to wear this gorgeous dress one more time!"

Marianne knew damn well that Elliott couldn't resist her sad puppy dog eyes. "Fine. I guess I can squeeze my balls into these pants for one more night."

"That's the spirit!" Odette said.

Lucien doubled over with laughter.

***

After the gallery was locked up for the night, Marianne headed to Odette's apartment to watch *Love Actually* with her—a weird tradition of theirs that Elliott wanted nothing to do with—and Lucien turned up at the studio apartment with an unopened bottles of champagne. They sat around cross-legged on the bed and drank the champagne from plastic tumblers. Elliott drank a little too much a little too fast. There was a pleasant buzzing in his skull by the time he'd finished his second cup.

"What's the deal with you and Ned Ferrars?" he asked suddenly. "Like, um, why does it have to be a secret?"

A part of him didn't know why he even asked the question. Another part of him was afraid it was because he wanted to believe it was a sham, that whatever Ned and Lucien had, it wasn't *real*. As though somehow that would make what had happened between Elliott and Ned at Norland Park something *true*. He hated that he still wanted that.

Lucien sighed. "His family is the *worst*, you know?"

"I know." Elliott suppressed a shudder as he thought of Francesca. "Ugh."

"Well," Lucien said, "when I finished my shitty degree in business administration, I landed in the city with nothing but a debt the size of a small planet, and I managed to score a summer internship with the Ferrars Corporation. And let me tell you, the only thing I learned there was how much I *hated* the construction industry." He grimaced. "Just, no."

Elliott took another sip of champagne.

"But I met Ned." A fond smile tugged at the corners of Lucien's mouth, and Elliott felt a pang of hateful jealousy in his gut. "We started having these lunch dates. Except I didn't really know they were lunch dates. Just he would always be at the deli at the same time as me, and we ended up eating on the same bench in the park? I mean, I don't think he knew they were lunch dates either?" His smiled broadened. "He's socially awkward, and super shy."

Was he? Elliott felt a jolt of guilt rush through him. If Ned was shy, then had Elliott pushed him in some way? He didn't remember it like that. He remembered a sort of strange, almost magnetic attraction that neither of them had resisted. What if it hadn't been like that at all though? What if Elliott had been the one who'd initiated things?

"So that went on for a few weeks, and then my nonna dropped dead."

"Oh!"

"It was years ago." Lucien waved his hand, slopping a little champagne onto the comforter. "Whoops. Anyway, I was a mess. Like, lost metro card levels of mess."

Elliott smiled at that, and held the bottle out to top up Lucien's champagne.

"And Ned was really sweet, and really kind." Lucien exhaled slowly. "He was . . . wow. I don't even know how to say it. He was everything I needed."

Elliott's chest tightened. Yeah. Yeah, he knew that feeling.

"So we started dating for real. Then, three years ago, he proposed to me on New Year's Eve. Only his mother is still living in denial and wants him to bring him a nice girl, so it's kind of . . ." He waved his hand again, and then snorted. "We don't see each other much because he's away so often. It's like, we're together, even if we're not *together*. It's complicated. It's weird, I guess, but also, it works. It's nice, you know? Comfortable." His forehead creased in a frown. "I mean, I think it works?"

He made it sound like a question, and Elliott fought down the sudden rush of stupid hope. Because if Lucien wasn't sure, then *maybe* . . .

Stupid.

Even if Lucien and Ned weren't perfect, even if there was space between them . . . well, Elliott had no right to imagine himself in that space. No right at all.

"Opposites attract, right?" Lucien's smile was tentative. "Like, even when he's in the city he doesn't like to go out and *do* things, but that's okay, right? We don't have to like the same stuff." He picked at his thumbnail. "He's *sweet*."

Elliott had never heard the word sound so . . . lacking. He looked away briefly.

Lucien sighed. "You know, I always said I wouldn't date anyone who was still in the closet, because I'm not here for that shit, but Ned's *not* in the closet. His family just keeps trying to push him back in there. Ned wants to give them time. I think that maybe if they *met* me? I mean, I think I'm likeable?"

"You are," Elliott said, his throat dry. "You're likeable."

"Stop trying to make me fall in love with you," Lucien chided. He drew a deep breath. "So anyway, that's my messy love life. What's yours like?"

"Non-existent," Elliott said firmly.

"Aw, how can that even be true?" Lucien patted him on the cheek. "You're adorable."

I'm a terrible person, Elliott wanted to tell him. *I didn't know, but I did a terrible thing.*

"I guess I'm socially awkward and super shy too," he said instead, and Lucien laughed.

"You and Ned would get on great!" he exclaimed, delighted, and Elliott hated himself just that little bit more.

***

Elliott stumbled out of bed and weaved his way toward the bathroom. It was still dark. The middle of the night, probably. Marianne was snoring on the bed, and Lucien was sleeping on the couch, and somehow there were more empty bottles on the counter than they'd started with.

Elliott pissed, sighing with relief as he relieved the pressure on his bladder, and then washed his hands and headed back to bed.

Something was buzzing.

Elliott blinked around for a while, his still-drunk brain taking a moment to put the pieces together. Then he saw the cell phone sitting on the floor. He stooped down to pick it up—it took two tries—and then squinted at the screen.

Ned.

His heart leapt, and his stomach fluttered with anticipation.

And then he realized.

This wasn't his phone. It was Lucien's. Ned was calling Lucien.

Elliott set the phone down on the small table beside the bed, and climbed back under the comforter with Marianne. He squeezed his stinging eyes shut and waited for sleep.

CHAPTER 16

Five was exactly how Elliott had imagined. It was full of so much glass—mirrors and chandeliers and entire wall panels—that it felt more like a sideshow maze than an actual restaurant. There were candles on the tables. Everything shone and glittered ad infinitum. Or ad nauseam. Elliott wasn't sure yet.

They wended their way through the tables, following their server. The other diners were dressed immaculately. The plates were large and square. The meals were small. Light bounced off wine glasses and silver cutlery and jewelry. The soft strains of a string quartet floated out above the low murmur of conversation broken only by the occasional braying laugh.

Heads turned here and there as they walked to their table, and Elliott didn't flatter himself that they were for anyone but Marianne. She looked resplendent in her green halter-neck dress. She looked older than eighteen. A woman, not a teenager. She *was*, Elliott supposed, but he was unused to seeing her as these people must: a *vision*. Marianne was too loud, too outspoken, too invested in the world and the people in it to be something as shallow, as fleeting, as a vision.

Lucien pulled out her chair for her, and Marianne swept her hands under her ass as she sat.

Elliott pulled out Odette's chair, and then sat beside her.

Their server introduced himself, handed out menus, and ran through the chef's recommendations of the day. Elliott felt a sudden rush of homesickness for the restaurant back in Barton Lake, where the floor was a little scuffed and the décor was tired, but a man could live on a serving of carbonara for half a day.

"I'll give you a few moments to decide," the server said, and melted away again.

"You know, back when your father was just starting out and came into the city, I used to take him to dinner," Odette said. She curled her crimson mouth in a smile. "People who didn't know him used to assume he was my boy toy. Didn't he love that?"

Elliott smiled at the thought. His dad would have loved that. He would have had fun with it, played it up, and then rushed home to tell Abby all about it.

"You look a lot like him," Odette said. She patted his arm. "Of course, one thing Henry was good at was producing beautiful kids."

Marianne smiled, delighted.

"Thank you," Elliott said, reaching for the glass of sparkling water. "For . . . for everything you've done for us. Not just these past few weeks, but always."

Odette raised her eyebrows. "Oh, I'm not done with you lot yet. I've already told you. In a few years I'll be back to see what Greta's doing. That girl is going to be something amazing, whatever she turns her hand to."

"At this point we just hope it's something legal," Marianne said.

Their server returned to take their orders.

Elliott glanced around at the other patrons from time to time. He had been privileged to grow up in Norland Park, in all senses of the word. But they'd never been like their neighbors. They'd never been like the Family. There was a difference between privileged and elitist, wasn't there? Elliott hoped there was.

Was it even fair to judge the other patrons like that? Maybe there were more Odettes in the crowd than Aunt Cynthias. Maybe making assumptions about them just for being wealthy was narrow-minded and unreasonable. Then again, maybe they were rich New York assholes and deserved as much judgment as Elliott could sling at them.

And this was why Elliott needed to get back to Barton Lake, get back to work, and get back to concentrating on his own life instead of anyone else's.

He sipped his water and listened to Lucien talk about some new up and coming artist that Odette had discovered.

The art world was a strange intersecting point where wealth met poverty. Elliott knew from handling Henry's business affairs for the past few years that even Henry—gifted but not a prodigy, known but not famous—barely made a living wage. If not for the grudging charity from the Family in the form of his monthly stipend and the house, their circumstances would have been very different. Sometimes Elliott had watched his dad paint, and he'd thought of all those other people out there, the people who had to kill their passion slowly and work their everyday jobs, because they didn't have Henry Dashwood's privilege. How odd that art was valued by the rich, but artists weren't.

Yeah. Elliott needed to go home.

And Barton Lake could be home, if he worked at it.

Their meals arrived, and they ate. The food was fine. Elliott felt a little like he did when he walked around Odette's gallery: out of his depth when it came to understanding the difference between the work of an artist and an artisan. He would have been as happy eating at the deli.

He was quiet, content to listen to the conversation float around him. He remembered Abby fretting about his shyness when he was a kid, but it had never really been shyness.

"He's fine," his dad had said, winking at Elliott. *"Aren't you, kiddo?"*

"Yes!"

Henry had ruffled his hair gently. *"You're a watcher, Elliott. A thinker. A Thoreau in the woods, living deliberately."*

"Yes," Elliott had agreed, although he'd been seven or eight and had no idea what his dad was talking about. He'd liked the phrase though. Living deliberately. He'd liked the idea that there was a purpose to the way he was, not a deficiency like his mom worried.

Elliott wanted to go back to Barton Lake and live deliberately. Practically. Purposefully.

He stabbed a spear of asparagus and smiled as Lucien made some joke. He was already halfway home to Barton Lake in his mind. Already letting New York go. Already thinking of that squeaky sofa bed and all his belongings stacked onto the bookshelf. The tiny little bathroom, the table that didn't sit all of them at once. The store downstairs. The smell of incense. The battalions of tiny crystal figures. The yoga DVDs. Barton Lake wasn't quite home yet, but Elliott felt it tugging gently at the core of him, urging him back.

The sudden clatter of cutlery pulled him out of his reverie.

"Mar?" He looked sharply at her.

Marianne ignored her dropped fork. She rose from her seat, eyes wide and mouth open. And then a sudden, brilliant smile lit up her face. "Jack!" A breathless laugh. "Jack!"

Elliott turned.

A server was navigating a couple through the tables. A pretty blonde woman in a red dress, and Jack. Jack Willoughby. He had an arm behind the woman, a hand on her hip, guiding her.

Elliott interpreted that, he thought later, long before Marianne did.

"Jack!" Marianne called, stepping away from the table to meet him.

No, Elliott thought. *No, Mar.*

He'd always been the pessimist, hadn't he? Or the realist. Or maybe he'd always known that Marianne would one day fly too close to the sun, and that her wings would melt and she would fall. And she was. In this moment she was already falling, the earth rushing up too fast to meet her, except she didn't even realize yet.

Elliott pushed his chair back and stood.

"Jack!" Marianne stood in front of him, in front of the woman he was with, and her smile didn't even waver. Not then. Not yet. "Jack, I thought you weren't in the city!"

Because she was so honest, because she was so open—because she was *Marianne* . . . Elliott's heart clenched and he took a step before her. Because it would never occur to her to lie, Marianne didn't see one when it was standing right in front of her, but Elliott saw it.

"I thought you were in Chicago!"

He saw it in the way the guilt flashed across Jack's face. He saw it in the way his hand hovered above the blonde woman's hip before settling there again decisively. He saw it in the way Jack squared his shoulders and looked Marianne up and down as though she were nothing more than a stranger to him.

"Marianne," he said at last. There was no warmth in his expression. "What are you doing here?"

"Jack, what . . ." Marianne trailed off, her smile finally faltering as she glanced at the woman, and then back to Jack. "Who is this?"

"Charlotte," Jack said, his expression cold. "My fiancée."

"Your . . ." Marianne shook her head. "I don't understand."

Jack's mouth tightened into a thin line for a moment before he spoke again. "Lose my number," he said, and ushered the woman past her.

Marianne turned to follow him.

Elliott caught her by the wrist. "Mar, no. Let's go. Let's just go."

Marianne stared at him, her gaze searching his as though she were seeking understanding. As though she were begging him not to ruin her whole world. Elliott had only seen that expression on her face once before. It was when their dad had explained that his treatment was no longer working. That he was dying.

"Elliott," Marianne had whispered then, and whispered now. "Elliott?"

"Let's go," he urged her in a low voice. "Let's go outside."

He led her through the tables, burning with hatred for Jack Willoughby and for every fucking person who stared at her humiliation. Tears slid down Marianne's face as he drew her toward the exit.

The *maître d'* held the doors open and ushered them into the cold night air. Elliott pulled Marianne down the sidewalk, away from the wide windows of the restaurant. Stopped in front of brickwork, and bracketed her against it with his arms.

Traffic, horn blasts, and sirens at his back.

Fingers of cold air tugged at his hair, slid down the collar of his shirt, but Elliott barely noticed them. He kept his gaze fixed on Marianne's pale face.

A hundred emotions flitted over her features, none settling long enough for Elliott to name. At last she drew in a shaking, rasping breath, her bottom lip trembling.

"Elliott . . ." Her mouth fell open. "Elliott, what just happened?"

"I don't know," he said numbly. "I don't know."

Because love is bullshit, Mar.

Because love is a lie.

Because I don't know.

I don't know.

Elliott had seen, though, hadn't he? He'd seen the way Jack looked at her. The way they'd laughed and kissed and brightened the world around them. Maybe something so big, so bright, was always fated to crash and burn. But that cold, blank stare Jack had levelled at Marianne . . . Love like that was supposed to end in heartbreak if it went wrong, wasn't it? In fiery wreckage, not in ice.

Elliott looked back toward the restaurant. Odette and Lucien were hurrying toward them, coats bundled in their arms.

"I just . . ." Marianne pressed a hand to her mouth. "I just need to talk to him, to—"

"No. Marianne, no."

"It's a mistake," Marianne said, determination creeping back into her tone. She pushed him away gently. "If I can just talk to him, he can tell me it's a mistake."

"Marianne!" Elliott reached out for her again, and she dodged away. "Mar!"

"It was a mistake," she said firmly, backing away from him.

And then she was standing right on the edge of the sidewalk. And then her heel was slipping, catching against the gutter, and she was falling backward into the street.

Traffic. Horn blasts. Sirens.

A screech of brakes.

The dull thud of impact.

Odette screaming.

***

The waiting room smelled of antiseptic.

Elliott's phone shook in his hand as he tried to unlock it.

Odette's hand curled around his, and she plucked the phone from him. "Let me do it, sweetheart."

Elliott nodded, numb.

He sank back into his chair and stared at his feet. Lucien was sitting beside him, a hand curled around the back of Elliott's neck. He'd been sitting like that for what felt like hours now, but maybe it hadn't been that long. Elliott didn't know. His arm must have been getting tired though.

A dumb thing to think. Stupid. But his brain was seizing on the most random stuff, trying to get a fix on something. Caught in the dizzying whirl of a maelstrom, searching desperately for an anchor.

Elliott had been in too many hospitals lately.

Made too many horrible calls.

"Mom? Mom, it's Elliott. You and the girls need to get here now. It's Dad. He's . . . he's going."

It was a strange way to say it, but Elliott hadn't known how else to phrase it. He's *dying*? He'd been dying for months. Stupid, useless, clumsy words.

What was he supposed to say?

There would be no asking for her to get here this time. No telling her to hurry; Abby was on the other side of the country. She might as well have been on the other side of the world. And he couldn't . . . He couldn't bring himself to crush her with another phone call, and so, like a coward, he let Odette do the talking.

Odette handed his phone back when she was done.

Elliott reached for the forms lying on the spare seat beside him and clutched them to his chest. He stood up and scrolled through his contacts. The number rang and rang, and just when Elliott thought nobody was going to answer, someone did.

"Elliott?"

"Hey, John."

John's voice sharpened. "What's wrong?"

"Marianne got hit by a car." Elliott walked away from the chairs. Stood by the potted palm in the corner. "I'm at the hospital. Can you come here? We don't have insurance, John. I need you to tell them you'll pay."

"Jesus, Elliott." For a moment there was silence, and then he spoke again: "Is Marianne okay?"

"I don't know." His voice cracked. "She's still in surgery."

"Okay," John said. "Okay, I can't get there, but put me on the phone to whoever needs my details, okay?"

Elliott felt a sudden jab of guilt. "We're in New York."

"What?"

"We're at Mount Sinai Beth Israel."

"Shit. Hang on a second."

Elliott heard him talking to someone in the background. Francesca, probably. He closed his eyes and drew in a deep breath. "John?"

"Yeah. Yeah, I'm here. I'll be there in about an hour, okay? Is anyone with you?"

"Yeah. Yeah, Odette is here."

"The art lady?"

"Yeah." Elliott put his hand on the wall. Tried to brace himself somehow. "You're coming?"

"I'm on my way."

"Thank you." Elliott's hand shook. "Please hurry."

Odette appeared at his side as he ended the call, and steered him back to his seat.

***

Elliott watched as people came and went. Doctors and nurses. A janitor dragging a mop in a wheeled bucket. He watched the television on the wall. There was no volume, and he didn't bother reading the subtitles. Just watched the people on the screen. Talking. Driving. Laughing. Eating. Smiling. It all seemed oddly mechanical, as if they were a cheap facsimile of reality, or Elliott had been somehow jolted out of step with the rest of the universe.

Odette spent a lot of time on the phone with Abby, reassuring her because Elliott was too numb to do it. Lucien brought him a coffee that slowly turned cold.

Waiting was the worst, people always said.

That wasn't true.

What came after the waiting might be the worst.

Elliott looked up as the elevator doors at the end of the corridor rolled open.

It wasn't John Dashwood.

It was someone so unexpected that for a moment Elliott just stared, unsure of how to make sense of it.

Colonel Deanna Brandon strode forward, her gait customarily stiff, her mouth pressed into a thin line. She stopped in front of Elliott. Her eyes were dark with worry.

"Paula called me," she said. "What do you need?"
Elliott stared up at her wordlessly.

CHAPTER 17

"I fucking hate hospitals," Deanna said some time later, feeding coins into the coffee machine.

"Yeah." Elliott glanced back to where Lucien and Odette were sitting. Odette had filled Deanna in on what had happened, including the confrontation in the restaurant with Jack. Deanna had looked horrified. "Me too."

Hospitals. His dad. Sitting and waiting for him to die.

Coffee began to dribble into the paper cup.

"My adopted daughter," Deanna said. "There's a story there."

Elliott met her gaze.

"When I was going through basic, I fell in love with my instructor," Deanna said bluntly. "This was in the Don't Ask, Don't Tell days. My instructor was a woman. Lizzie. She was my first love. She was older than me, straight, and married. Married to an abusive asshole." Her expression tightened. "She left the service and we lost contact. Years later I discovered she'd dumped the asshole, but she'd been dealing with some other stuff too. She'd been in an accident. Back injury. She got addicted to opioids. Then, once she couldn't get a doctor to prescribe them anymore, she moved onto meth."

Elliott nodded, even though he was unsure of the point of the story.

Deanna wrestled her cup free from the machine. She sipped her coffee, and her mouth turned down at the corners. "Tastes like shit."

"Yeah."

Deanna turned and dumped the entire cup in the trash. "Anyway, Lizzie had a daughter. Eliza. I adopted her when Lizzie passed. It wasn't perfect. I was still on active duty then, and maybe I wasn't home enough. And Eliza had her own issues, thanks to her mom. Five years ago I got home from deployment, and Eliza tells me she got pregnant. She was sixteen, and the guy drove her to a clinic to get an abortion, and left her there. Didn't even stick around to drive her home again."

"Shit."

"She begged me not to go to the police and have him charged with statutory." Deanna's expression darkened. "She still loved him. And I didn't want to put her through that. Maybe I should have. I don't know. But she was so fragile, and it would have been the biggest scandal to hit Barton Lake since your dad ran away with the nanny."

"Shit," Elliott said again, his stomach churning as the pieces fell into place.

"Yeah," Deanna said. "Jack Willoughby."

Elliott exhaled heavily.

"I thought he'd changed," Deanna said. "I'm sorry."

"Even if you'd said something, she wouldn't have believed you. I wouldn't have either."

"Yeah." Deanna grimaced. "I know."

"Is Eliza okay?" Elliott asked quietly.

"She's doing well." Deanna's smile appeared grudging yet genuine. "She has a good group of friends now. A good support system."

Elliott nodded.

Deanna held his gaze. "Marianne's going to be okay, Elliott. She's going to be okay."

Elliott nodded again, and they went back to wait with Odette and Lucien.

***

John Dashwood arrived at the hospital with Francesca in tow. Elliott was surprised, and grateful, to find himself enfolded into a hug.

"Thank you for coming," Elliott said, his chest aching. "Thank you."

"Hey." John leaned back long enough to meet Elliott's gaze before hugging him again. "She's my sister too."

Elliott's eyes stung with sudden tears, and he held John tighter while he fought them. All this time, all these years, had John *wanted* to be their brother in more than name? Or had Henry's death shaken something loose in him, made him reach out for some reason when the rest of the Family had pushed them away? Had it taken burying his father for John to want to know his siblings?

John was still holding him close when the surgeon appeared to talk to them.

"You're all family?" she asked, looking around the room.

Elliott nodded. Close enough. He couldn't help but look at the surgeon's hands, and wonder how steady they were, how competent.

"Okay," the surgeon said. "Marianne's out of surgery. She's in an induced coma at the moment, just until the swelling on her brain goes down. We'll bring her around in a few hours, and we're hopeful she'll respond well and there's no injury to the brain itself. In pedestrian accidents, it's common to see trauma to the head, pelvis, and legs. In Marianne's case her right leg is fractured in several places, and our concern there was internal bleeding, but she's come out of surgery really well."

Really well. Elliott's brain seized on that hopefully.

"Now, it was a low speed collision, so there's no fractures to the pelvic area." The surgeon smiled. "The CT scans also didn't show any spinal injuries, so, barring a brain injury, I'm hopeful the worst of it is her leg. We've inserted pins to set the fractures, and we'll reassess in a few days, but she's doing very well."

"Can I see her?" Elliott asked.

"I'll have a nurse come and get you when you can go in."

"Thank you. So I can call our mom and say she's going to be okay?"

"Barring any potential brain injuries, yes."

"What are the chances of that?" Elliott asked. "Of brain injuries?"

"That's very much a wait and see scenario. I know that's a frustrating answer for you, but we'll know more in a few hours."

"Okay," Elliott said. "Thank you."

The surgeon nodded and left the waiting area.

"That's good, right?" Elliott asked.

John patted his back. "Yeah, that's good. Do you want to call Abby and tell her, or do you want me to do it?"

"I don't know." Elliott felt like he was caught in limbo. While his initial sharp fear had flooded away, it had been replaced now by something different. By a more insidious sort of worry. It was like a precarious balancing act. Marianne wasn't going to die, which was good. Obviously it was fucking good. But Abby would ask how bad it was, and what was Elliott supposed to say? Because they didn't know yet. Maybe it would be good, probably it would be good, but probably wasn't a guarantee. There had been a time when Henry's prognosis had been optimistic too, until time and experience had worn all that away into the awful, stark reality of *"I'm sorry, Henry. There's nothing else we can do."* Elliott didn't want that again. He wasn't sure he could deal with that again. He needed something definite.

John was still waiting for his answer.

"I'll do it," Elliott said. "I'll call Mom."

Because in the end it didn't matter how unsteady the ground was underneath Elliott's feet. He had to step up anyway.

***

It was late by the time a nurse came to show Elliott and John to Marianne's room. She looked so pale, lying in the hospital cot, hooked up to machines and monitors, with a breathing tube in her throat and a cannula in the back of her hand. Pale, but with a stark black bruise on her cheek, her skin scoured where she'd hit the street. Her right leg was elevated in traction. There was a complicated brace around it, almost like a cage, with metal pins digging in through the bandages. Elliott wondered how far those pins went, and then decided he didn't want to think about it.

"Hey, Mar," he said softly, and took a seat beside the bed. He put his hand gently over hers, careful not to jostle the cannula.

John sat on the other side of the bed.

They were silent for a long while, listening to Marianne's heart monitor beep away.

"I didn't even know you guys were in New York," John said at last.

"Sorry." Elliott looked at Marianne to avoid having to meet John's gaze. "There's an exhibit of Dad's work. Odette asked us to come."

"I knew she was putting something together. She wanted a bunch of his stuff."

"It's still on," Elliott said. "If you want to see it."

John snorted softly.

Of course Elliott hadn't been the only one to notice how Henry's work didn't include John. How his photographs and diary entries didn't. If Elliott had felt like an imposter at the gallery, then John would have felt like an interloper.

He rubbed his thumb gently over the back of Marianne's hand. "I'm sorry."

"It doesn't matter." John shook his head. "Art's not my thing."

"Mine neither," Elliott said.

John lifted his gaze from Marianne. "What is your thing, Elliott?"

There was no malice behind the question. No barb. Just an honest curiosity that Elliott had no idea how to answer. He felt tired. Wrung out. Stripped bare. He felt alone.

"I don't know," he said at last, curling his fingers around Marianne's. "I don't think I've found it yet."

***

The hours passed slowly back in the waiting room.

Francesca's heels clicked across the floor as she headed over toward the coffee machine. She punched at the buttons and glanced over at Elliott. Her mouth was pursed into a thin, unhappy line, and Elliott figured that yeah, okay, the last time she'd seen him he'd had her brother's dick in his hand, but still. He wondered why she was even here. To support John, or to make sure he didn't do something stupid and write Elliott a blank check?

Probably the second one.

Elliott sat for a while, and then paced for a while, and then sat again. Lucien stood up to leave at one point, whispering an apology as he hugged Elliott tightly, but someone had to open the gallery in the morning.

It was strange. Elliott felt that the entire world should have paused and held its breath at a time like this. Just like it should have when Henry died. But the world didn't stop for tragedy. People still had jobs, and bills to pay, and the wheels kept on turning.

"I'll come back later," Lucien promised. "Text me if you need me to bring anything."

Lucien had already done so much for them. His friendship, his lunch dates, his—

"Your friend's dress," Elliott said. "It's ruined."

"Don't," Lucien said, squeezing him tighter. ""Don't even worry about some dumb dress."

Middle-of-the-night television was terrible. Elliott watched it anyway, tensing whenever he heard some incomprehensible announcement over the hospital PA system. Elliott wasn't the only person here who wanted to world to stop turning long enough so he could find his feet again, was he? He wasn't the only one standing numbly while a storm broke around him. The same story was being played out all over the hospital, all throughout the city, the country and the world.

It was morning when the surgeon came back and told them that Marianne was awake.

Elliott hurried to her room.

She looked awful and wonderful at the same time. Her bruises appeared even more stark this morning, and there were black shadows under her eyes. Her hair was messy and lank, but she was alive. She was alive, and she knew her name and the date, and the president, and the surgeon said there was no sign of any brain injury.

"Elliott," she said, her voice tripping over the syllables of his name. "My head hurts."

"Yeah." Elliott brushed her hair gently off her forehead. "The doctor said if you press this button you get morphine."

"Ooooh." Marianne pressed the button. "Huh. I'm not really feeling it."

"That's because it's supposed to make you stop hurting, not get high."

"That's no fun." Her dozy smile faded. "I'm really tired."

"I know." Elliott squeezed her hand gently.

John stood in the doorway watching. He looked tired. Maybe relieved. Maybe even a little envious.

"John," Marianne said in a wondering tone that Elliott thought had something to do with her concussion, and something to do with her morphine. "Hi!"

"Hi," he said awkwardly, straightening up.

"Come here," Marianne said.

John exchanged a look with Elliott before moving inside the room and taking a seat beside the bed.

"I got hit by a car," Marianne told him.

"I heard," John said, reaching out to take her hand.

"It really hurt." Marianne wrinkled her nose. "But now I have morphine."

"Good." John looked to be fighting a smile. "Morphine is good."

"Morphine is . . ." Marianne dozed off again before she could finish her sentence.

Elliott held her hand for a while after.

***

The following days were a blur. Elliott spent as much time as he could at Mount Sinai, and the rest of his time catching up on sleep in the apartment above the studio. John joined him at the hospital for at least a few hours a day, and Elliott was grateful. He wasn't sure he could deal with everything on his own, particularly when Abby was frantically calling at least four or five times a day, worrying that she needed to be there for Marianne. Elliott suspected that Paula and Deanna were running some interference on his behalf there, or Abby would have been calling at least twice as often.

Even Francesca made visits to the hospital. Elliott didn't know if she was finally starting to soften to him and Marianne, or if perhaps she didn't trust John not to welcome them into the bosom of the Family without her there to stop him. If her frosty presence was the price he had to pay for finally beginning to forge a relationship with his brother, that was fine.

Marianne was recovering well. By the end of the week she was in discussions with her surgeon as to the best way of getting home to California. Her surgeon was happy to transfer into the care of a doctor closer to home, but didn't want her flying so soon after surgery with the increased risk of blood clots. She wanted to wait another week or two, but Marianne hated being stuck in hospital, and hated being stuck in New York. Elliott couldn't blame her. Their trip had ended in disaster, and they both wanted to put it behind them.

It was Deanna who came up with the idea of hiring a van. They could share the driving, and make Marianne as comfortable as possible in the back seat. Elliott shuddered at the thought of another drive all the way to California, but Marianne looked so hopeful that he didn't dismiss it out of hand.

Elliott was heading into the hospital one afternoon with Lucien at his side when it happened. He was punching the button for the elevator when he heard someone call his name from behind.

"Elliott!"

Elliott turned and saw Jack Willoughby standing there, a bunch of flowers in his hand. A fucking bunch of flowers. The sheer fucking audacity of it froze Elliott for a moment.

Jack looked shamefaced. He looked miserable, like he hadn't been sleeping.

Good.

Fucking *good*.

"You take one more step toward Marianne's room, and I'll punch you in the fucking face," Elliott said.

"Elliott, please, let me explain." Jack's voice was raw.

Elliott folded his arms over his chest. He didn't take his eyes off Jack. Beside him, Lucien squared his shoulders, like maybe this really was going to end in a fight. Elliott had never punched anyone before in his life. He abhorred violence, but he was willing to make an exception in Jack's case.

"My . . . my aunt," Jack said. He dragged his fingers through his hair. "She threatened to cut me off. I . . . I *love* Marianne, but . . ." He shrugged helplessly. "You understand, right?"

"Yeah," Elliott said. "I understand. You chose money over my sister."

Jack flinched.

"You walked into our house, and you called yourself our friend, and you chose the money." Elliott shook his head. "Get the hell out of here, Jack."

Jack held the flowers out. "Will you . . . will you give them to her?"

Lucien stepped forward and snatched the bouquet out of his hand. Then he strode to the nearest trash can and thrust them inside. "You heard him," he said, dusting the pollen off his hands. "Get out of here."

Jack nodded dumbly. He shoved his hands into the pockets of his expensive jeans and then turned and walked away.

He looked like a broken man.

Elliott fought down the wave of sympathy that rose up in him. Because he knew what people like that were like. He knew what it was to have a Family instead of a family. He knew that not everyone could make the same decision that Henry Dashwood had.

But meanwhile, Marianne was lying upstairs in a hospital bed.

Jack Willoughby was a broken man?

Good.

CHAPTER 18

On his last morning in New York, Elliott packed his and Marianne's bags and looked around the small apartment that had been home for longer than he'd intended. There were things he'd miss about the city, but it had mostly been a disaster. Not a total disaster—he and John talked every day now, which was nice—but Marianne's heartbreak and humiliation had been too high a price to pay for that. It was too high a price to pay for anything, Elliott thought. They'd both had their dreams crushed in the city, hadn't they? Marianne on that awful night, and Elliott because of Lucien. And maybe Marianne's dream had been bigger, brighter, a riot of beautiful color, but Elliott's, cautious and small-drawn, hadn't been nothing.

Marianne was waiting downstairs for him now. Elliott and Odette had collected her from the hospital an hour ago because she'd insisted she wanted to see the Retrospective again before she left and take photographs for Abby and Greta. Elliott had left her on a chair in front of one of the display cases while he came upstairs to pack, and Lucien darted around snapping pictures on his phone.

The Henry Dashwood Retrospective still had a few weeks to run, but many of the paintings had already been sold and would be shipped off to their new owners once the exhibit closed. Odette hadn't figured out their cut on the merchandising yet, but with the painting alone they were looking at around sixty thousand dollars. Henry would have been proud.

"They'll be worth a hell of a lot more when I'm dead. Make sure they pay through the nose, Elliott!"

And they had.

Sixty thousand seemed like a lot, but Elliott was conscious that was it now; there would be no more paintings to sell. That money needed to stretch a long way into the future. But it was a safety net, and it was a weight off his shoulders. It was breathing room.

Elliott looked around the apartment one last time, then slung their bags over his shoulder and took the service elevator downstairs to the gallery. He got off at the second floor and glanced at Marianne. She looked tired, but she was as eager as Elliott to put New York behind them.

Elliott stood in front of *Abigail in Lamplight* and smiled at her. In a few months she'd be back in California, propped against the wall behind Abby's bed where she belonged.

Footsteps sounded on the stairs, and Elliott turned in time to see John and Francesca stepping into the room. Francesca immediately averted her gaze from *Abigail in Lamplight* and huffed a breath.

John came to stand beside Elliott. "This painting still horrifies me."

"Oh, please," Elliott said, elbowing him. "It's not *your* mom's vulva."

"Thank God."

Elliott smiled.

"So this is what he did, huh?" John said after a moment.

"Yeah," Elliott said softly.

John moved away to look at one of the display cases. Elliott watched him, only vaguely aware of the low sounds of a conversation behind him. John lifted a hand and traced his fingers over the glass above one of Henry's brushes, and Elliott wondered what the gesture meant to him. He wondered how it felt to lose his father twice.

"*What.*" Francesca's voice rose. "*What?*"

Elliott turned quickly, realization rushing over him as he saw Lucien standing in front of Francesca.

Oh, no. Lucien.

He remembered what Lucien had said the night after the opening, when they'd all drunk too much champagne: "*His family just keeps trying to push him back in there. Ned wants to give them time. I think that maybe if they met me? I mean, I think I'm likeable?*"

"What?" Francesca exclaimed again, her voice rising into something like a shriek. "John!"

Lucien backed away from her, his eyes wide.

"John!" Francesca pointed an accusatory finger at Lucien. "This . . . this *person* says that he's engaged to Ned!"

John stood there like a deer caught in headlights.

Elliott turned to look at Marianne. She was wide-eyed, a hand raised to cover her open mouth.

"John!" Francesca exclaimed again.

"Hey," Elliott said, crossing over to Lucien's side. "Francesca, just take a breath, okay?"

"You!" Francesca exclaimed. "Don't you *dare—*"

"Shut up." The last thing Elliott needed was for Francesca to spill about what he'd done with Ned. Lucien didn't deserve that. And Elliott wished he could pretend that sentiment came from a place of moral decency, but it didn't. It was selfish, too. He didn't want Lucien to hate him, and he didn't want to be humiliated again. "You need to shut the hell up. You're not Ned's keeper, and you and your evil fucking family should be over the moon to have someone like Lucien in it. He's a better person than the rest of you put together!"

He clamped his mouth shut, surprised at his own vehemence. The vaulted ceilings really projected his voice. Great acoustics. Much more volume than he'd intended.

Francesca gasped.

Lucien's jaw dropped.

John face-palmed.

Marianne raised her other hand to her mouth.

"John!" Francesca turned toward him, tearful. "John! Don't let him talk to me like that!"

John drew a deep breath. "Let's go, Frannie." He put an arm around her shoulders and steered her toward the stairs. "Elliott, drive safe. Marianne, you look after yourself. Call me when you get home."

Elliott nodded, stunned at his own outburst and at what he was almost certain was the rueful smile John was fighting to hide.

"What just happened?" Lucien whispered once John and Francesca had descended the stairs. "What did I *do*?"

"I think you'd better call Ned," Elliott said. "Before Francesca does."

"Oh God." Lucien pressed a hand to his forehead. "Oh my God."

"You're better than them. Don't let them make you forget that."

"Oh my God," Lucien whispered again, as Odette clattered up the stairs demanding to know what the fuck she'd just missed.

***

"You knew," Marianne said when the room had cleared. "Elliott, you *knew*."

Elliott leaned on the wall next to her chair. The gallery was quiet now. Empty of everything except the ghosts of Henry Dashwood and the detritus of his life. Elliott stared at a photograph of Norland Park. In the corner of the frame he could see the greenhouse on the croquet lawn. He could smell the loam, and taste the beer on Ned's lips as they kissed.

"You *knew* they were engaged!" Marianne's voice hitched. Her eyes were wide and filled with tears. "How long have you known?"

"Since our first night here." Elliott's throat ached, and he was afraid to swallow.

"Why didn't you *tell* me?" There was something accusatory in her tone now.

He fought the urge to squeeze his eyes shut, to escape her gaze somehow. "Because he asked me to keep it a secret."

"Elliott!" She sounded outraged, and Elliott didn't know if it was because he'd kept his word or because she was angry on his behalf over Ned. These were unchartered waters for Elliott. They were treacherous, deep and unknown. They flooded into the hollow space inside his chest, dark and cold, and Elliott was afraid he was drowning.

"It was just a thing." he forced himself to say. "With Ned. It didn't mean anything."

"But Ned likes *you*!" There was a note of childish insistence in Marianne's tone that made his stomach roil. "He can't marry Lucien!"

"What do you want, Mar?" he asked, fighting to keep the bitterness out of his voice. "Do you want him to treat Lucien the way Jack treated you?"

It was an unfair blow, and one that caused Marianne to flinch back. Her fingers fluttered at the edges of the loose button-up shirt she was wearing over her skirt. Then she lifted her chin, her old determination back. "I think that Ned should marry who he *loves*."

Love.

There was the word Elliott had never dared pin to all his strange, fluttering hopes—too solid and equivocal a word for the mass of uncertain and contradictory feelings that clambered for attention when Elliott thought of Ned. He couldn't face it now.

Elliott turned away, and found himself staring at a photograph of his parents. They were standing in the sunlight outside of Norland Park. They were barefoot, and both of them were laughing. Henry had his arm around Abby's waist. She was heavily pregnant.

Jesus. He'd known Ned for *days*. A thing like that—like *love*—couldn't happen in days, no matter what his parents had always told him. No matter what had happened for them. That wasn't how the world worked.

"I think," he said, attempting uselessly to gather his thoughts. He swallowed, and began again. "I think that Ned made Lucien a promise that he never made to me, and that he should honor that promise. And I hope that they'll be very happy together." He looked at the way the light caught on his parents' faces. "I think that the idea that your happiness depends on just one person is—"

Is seductive. Beguiling. *Bewitching*. It was the sort of fantasy that even Elliott wanted to sink into, to drown in, but it wasn't real. How could it be real?

He swallowed again. "Impossible."

"Elliott." Marianne's voice was soft. When he turned back to face her, her eyes were shining with tears and there was a strange half-smile on her face, as though she were looking at something hopeless and pitiful. "Why are you like this? Why do you do this to yourself? You're always so caught up with *practicalities*." She said the word like it disgusted her, and then her expression softened again. "Elliott, where is your *heart*?"

Elliott flinched back, a sudden wave of something too cold to be anger coursing through him. "My *heart*? What the hell do you know about my heart? For weeks it's been all about *you*, Mar, about you and Jack, and the whole time I've been sitting on this thing with Lucien and Ned, listening to Lucien tell me what a great guy he is." His eyes stung. "And every time he says it is like a punch in the guts, but I sat there and I listened and I smiled like nothing was wrong, and you didn't even fucking *notice*!"

And maybe that was the betrayal that hurt the most: that his sister and his best friend in the world hadn't seen how much he was hurting, and all because he didn't wear his heart on his sleeve like she did.

It didn't mean he didn't have one.

If Elliott was heartless, then what was breaking inside him right now?

Tears slid down Marianne's face, her breathing choppy as she struggled to contain them. And Elliott didn't know if she was crying because he'd raised his voice to her, or if she was upset at his heartbreak, or at hers, or if—most likely—she was tired and in pain and this was the last fucking straw.

He crossed over to her and knelt beside her chair. She leaned into his embrace, and he closed his eyes as she cried on his shoulder.

"I want to go home," she murmured, her breath hot. "I just want to go home."

"Me too," he whispered. That, at least, was something they could agree on. "Me too, Mar."

***

"Road trip!" Marianne exclaimed as Elliott and Deanna helped her from the sidewalk and into the van. She grimaced as she knocked her leg against the door. "Fuck."

"No complaining," Deanna said. "If it's hurting, at least it's still there."

Marianne looked nonplussed for a moment, and then she smiled. It might have been the first smile Elliott had seen on her face in the two weeks since the accident. Not counting her dozy morphine grins. "You're a real glass half full person, aren't you?"

"That I am," Deanna deadpanned. "That I am."

From the doorway of the gallery, Odette and Lucien watched anxiously.

It took a while to get Marianne situated. She sat in the very back, with her leg propped up carefully on the folded-down seat in front of her. She had a nest of pillows to support her, and everything she might need in easy reach: a water bottle, her meds, snacks, a few magazines, and her phone.

"Okay?" Elliott asked her once she was buckled in.

"Yes," Marianne said. "We're going to avoid every pothole and speed bump between here and California, right?"

"That's a plan." He laid her crutches down on the floor.

"Elliott, get up front here," Deanna said. "I'm gonna need a navigator to get us out of the city. New York traffic terrifies me, and I've landed choppers at Bagram under heavy fire."

Elliott flashed a smile at Marianne and climbed out of the van. He pulled the back door closed, and turned to Odette and Lucien.

"Drive safe," Odette said.

"We will."

Lucien hugged him tightly. "Come back and visit us soon, Dashwoods!"

Elliott forced a smile. "Take care of yourself, Lucien."

He meant it. It would have been so much easier to hate Lucien, but life was never that simple, was it?

He extricated himself from Lucien's hug and then climbed into the front passenger seat.

"Ready to go home?" Deanna asked him.

"Fuck yes," Elliott said. "More than ready."

***

It took seven days to get to California, with Elliott and Deanna sharing the driving between them. Marianne was a trooper. She slept a lot of the way, but every bump in the road seemed to bring her awake again. At the end of each day she was usually in more pain that she admitted. Elliott could see it in the tight line of her mouth. So could Deanna.

They spent an entire day in Salt Lake City because Marianne couldn't face the idea of getting into the van again. They stayed in their hotel instead, and watched television and ate takeout.

"Don't apologize," Deanna told Marianne when she made a tearful attempt at doing so. "I know it hurts."

Marianne wiped her face with the sleeves of her hoodie.

"Have you tried yoga?" Deanna asked. "I hear it's very good."

Marianne started at her wide-eyed for a moment before bursting into laughter.

Deanna was a godsend. Elliott couldn't have done it without her. Her gruff no-bullshit exterior was actually paper-thin. Underneath that she was one of the warmest people Elliott had ever met, and it was ridiculous it had taken this long to realize it. How many other people would volunteer to drive across the country just to help them out?

He called John from Salt Lake City. He called Lucien too, but Lucien didn't answer. Elliott fretted about that for hours, afraid that Lucien had found out about him and Ned and would hate him for it, but he got a text back a few hours later apologizing for having missed his call, and hoping he and Marianne were both almost home. Elliott wished they were too, but they still had a few more days to go.

"I hate New York," Marianne said, somewhere between Winnemucca and Mill City. The landscape on either side of the highway was arid and brown, dotted with scrubby bushes. There were low hills on the horizon, bald and featureless.

Deanna was driving.

Elliott turned around in his seat. He was sitting in the middle row, on the one seat that they hadn't folded down for Marianne. "Everything about it?"

"He broke my heart, Elliott," Marianne said. "I was so stupid. I believed everything he said, and he broke my heart."

He'd broken his own too, Elliott thought. And he deserved all the pain it brought him.

"I don't know what to tell you, Mar," he said, helpless.

"Fractures heal," Deanna said from the front seat. "All of them."

Marianne lifted her chin. "When?"

"When they're ready."

The days passed with the scenery. Nights were motel beds and fast food and aching muscles from hours of driving. When they crossed the state border into California, Barton Lake seemed at once so close and still so far away. He wanted to put all of New York behind him too. He wanted to return to his small life. To Abby and Greta. To the restaurant and the shop. To people he knew and trusted.

He was tired.

"New York did a number on you too, didn't it?" Deanna asked him frankly, still a few hours out of Barton Lake. "And I don't just mean Marianne getting hurt."

Elliott checked that Marianne was sleeping in the back. "Yeah. I thought I liked someone. I thought he liked me. And then I met his fiancé."

"Does Marianne know?"

"She knows what happened." Elliott stared out the windshield.

"But she doesn't know you got your heart broken as well?"

Elliott smiled despite himself. "No, she knows that as well."

Deanna glanced at him. "You're an odd one, Elliott Dashwood."

"I . . . I'm going to take that as a compliment?"

"You probably should." Her mouth quirked in a smile.

"Fucking rich people though," Elliott said with a sigh. "No offense."

"I'm not old money, Elliott. I got where I am because my parents worked every day of their lives. They started off with a tiny little grocery store in Fresno, which they built into a chain of eight stores before they sold it. And believe me, when they bought the house in Barton Lake, there wasn't single day someone didn't remind them they'd come from stacking cans on shelves. There are people like Jack Willoughby's aunt who think that not being born into money is some kind of moral failing." She snorted. "You know. Assholes."

Elliott smiled. "Yeah. Assholes."

They continued to drive.

***

"Marianne!" Abby cried out as the van pulled into the narrow back yard behind the apartment. She hurried down the steps. "Elliott! Oh, Mar! My poor baby!"

Elliott and Deanna helped Marianne out of the van and onto her crutches.

"Mom!" Marianne exclaimed.

Abby dashed across the yard to meet her, pulling her into a careful hug before pressing her hands to her cheeks to hold her still while she peppered her with kisses. "Oh, Mar!"

"Let her breathe, Mom," Elliott chided gently, tugging Abby away.

Abby hugged him tightly. "Oh, Elliott!"

Elliott looked over her shoulder to where Greta was dragging herself down the steps. She was scowling, but Elliott wasn't fooled for a second. "Get over here, Greta."

Greta burrowed into their hug. "You suck, Elliott. You were away too long, and you brought Mar back broken."

Marianne poked her with her crutch. "Hey. Where's my hug?"

Greta buried her face into Marianne's shoulder and burst into tears.

"Oh!" Marianne patted her back awkwardly. "Oh, Greta. I missed you too, monster."

Abby smiled warmly at Deanna. "Thank you so much, Colonel Brandon, for bringing my babies home."

Deanna suddenly looked as gruff as awkward as she had the first time Elliott had met her. She cleared her throat. "That's, um, that's not a problem, Mrs. Dashwood. And it's Deanna, please."

"Then you have to call me Abby!" Abby insisted. "Come inside, please. I'll make you some oolong tea."

Deanna looked pained. "I, ah, I don't know what that is."

Abby took her by the arm and led her toward the stairs. "You'll love it, I promise."

Elliott eyed the stairs, and then looked at Mar. "What do you think? Bridal carry or piggy back?"

"Piggy back," Marianne said decisively.

"Let's do it," Elliott said, bracing himself to lift her.

Greta followed them up the stairs, carrying Marianne's crutches.

***

Abby declared she was sleeping with Marianne while she recovered, in case she needed anything, so Greta took her room. She didn't stay there though. Elliott woke up on his first night home to find her crawling into bed with him.

"Don't steal all the blankets," he said.

Greta tugged on them aggressively for a moment, and pressed her cold feet against his calves.

"Greta!"

She slumped down in defeat, and they lay in silence for a while. And then Greta said, "Mom was really scared, you know?"

"Yeah," Elliott said. "Me too."

"Me too," Greta echoed. "Please don't go away again, Elliott."

Elliott caught her hand and squeezed it.

"When . . ." Greta sniffed. "When Dad died, when we didn't get there in time . . . I thought it was happening again. I thought Marianne was going to die, and I wouldn't get to see her again. When you called Mom she just collapsed. It was like someone cut her strings." Her voice wavered. "And I can't be *you*, Elliott. I can't keep her together like you do, like you did when Dad died."

Elliott's heart clenched. "Jesus, Greta, you don't have to. That's not your job, okay?"

"It's not your job either!" she hissed. "But you did it because someone had to! God knows Mom can't!"

Elliott froze. What could he say? That it wasn't fair? Maybe not, but it was true, and Greta was smart enough to have seen it. Elliott loved Abby with all his heart, but growing up he'd always secretly wished she were more like other moms. Like the moms of his friends from school, who were . . . *normal*? Because there were some things that the universe didn't just take care of. There were some things Elliott had to take care of instead.

"It's not your job," Elliott said again. "Let me take care of stuff, okay?"

"You shouldn't have to do that all on your own," Greta whispered.

"I'm not. I've got you and Mar. We're in this together, right?"

"Right. Just don't go away again, okay? Not for a while, anyway."

"I won't," Elliott promised.

It was an easy promise to make, because where the hell else did he have to go? Barton Lake was home now.

For better or for worse, it was home.

CHAPTER 19

Winter in Barton Lake was beautiful. Ball-freezingly cold, but beautiful. Elliott took to escaping the apartment and walking around the lake. It was too deep to freeze over, but mist clung to the water on the coldest of days. Mount Shasta vanished behind a shroud of clouds, and the world seemed incredibly close and quiet and small-drawn. There was snow. More that Elliott had expected—he was still struggling with all his old preconceptions about California being all about sunlight and surf—but not enough for the snow days Greta was hoping for.

John Middleton continued to hold his Friday night get-togethers on his back deck, which was warmed by large outdoor heaters. Marianne always claimed the warmest place. She was still on crutches, for another week at least, but she was getting increasingly impatient with them and spent a lot of time hopping from place to place, stopping and yelling out for help when she overexerted herself and had invariably left her crutches out of reach.

"Did you hear?" Paula asked one Friday night, pouring Elliott a glass of wine.

"Hear what?" Elliott asked.

"Ferrars Construction passed on the land," Paula said with a sigh.

"Oh, I'm sorry."

Paula sighed again. "It can't be helped. And he was so nice about it when I spoke to him. He apologized for taking so long to get back to me, but he'd only just got back from his honeymoon."

Elliott flinched and spilled his wine. He reached for a napkin to mop it up. "Shit. Sorry."

Marianne shot him a sharp look.

Paula topped up his glass again, and moved on to chat with

Deanna.

It had been a week or so since Elliott had texted Lucien, but Lucien hadn't mentioned anything about getting married. Elliott wondered if he should text him his congratulations. But what if Lucien had found out about Ned and Elliott? Elliott didn't want to step into metro card messy territory. Lucien was a friend, but that friendship had always been conditional, hadn't it? It had relied on Lucien not knowing the truth. The best thing Elliott could do was to step away and let Lucien and Ned live their lives. Elliott had his own life in Barton Lake.

He had his mom, and Marianne and Greta, and he was working more hours at the restaurant. He had his eye on a rental a few blocks away from Main Street that had three bedrooms and a small study that could easily be a fourth bedroom. The house was out of their budget for now—Elliott didn't want to dip into their savings—but he could save a deposit in a few more months, and if the restaurant could guarantee him a few more shifts per week, it was doable. They could move into a bigger place and still keep a safety net.

Elliott took his wine and went and sat next to Marianne. She leaned into him. They looked out at the lake.

"I heard what Paula said," Marianne said at last.

"It doesn't matter." Elliott didn't look at her. He couldn't. "It was never going to be anything between us."

Over at the edge of the verandah, Greta and Poppy were lining olive pits up along the top of the railing, and then flicking them out into the darkness.

"I was a fool, wasn't I?" Marianne asked at last.

"Hmm?"

"With Jack," Marianne said. "I was a fool."

Elliott hesitated.

"You can say it. I know I was."

"He was sorry," Elliott said at last. "Jack was. He came to the hospital. He brought flowers. I think he was heartbroken too."

"Sure." Marianne wrinkled her nose. "Heartbroken, but still engaged to someone else."

Elliott put an arm around her. "Yeah."

"I am a flower in a garden," Marianne announced, her smile bright. "I am learning and I am growing."

"Have you been reading the magazines in the shop again?"

"Shut up." Marianne poked him in the ribs. "Don't mock my emotional journey."

"I would never."

Marianne leaned her head on his shoulder. "Also, I'm pretty sure I'm bi."

"Uh huh," Elliott said. "Did you figure that out all on your own?"

Marianne lifted her head and looked at him. Her face was pink, and Elliott wasn't sure it was entirely the fault of the heaters. "It's true what they say about yoga," she said at last. "It really does do amazing things for flexibility."

"You haven't been doing yoga," Elliott said, nodding at the cast on her leg.

"Deanna has," Marianne said. Maybe it was supposed to be a joke, but she wasn't smiling. She was waiting for Elliott's reaction, he realized, and for a moment, he wasn't sure what to think.

Deanna was older. There was a massive gulf of life experience there—probably a solid two decades at least. But their dad had been fifteen years older than their mom, so Elliott knew that for the right people, an age gap didn't matter. It didn't automatically translate into a power imbalance. And Deanna had volunteered to drive across the entire fucking continent just so Marianne could make it home earlier. She was a good person—Elliott didn't doubt that for a second—and maybe, for Marianne, Deanna was also the *right* person.

Marianne's revelation wasn't a total surprise. She had been spending a lot time with Deanna over the past few weeks, and wearing a sort of a secret smile whenever she got home again. It was unlike Marianne to play her cards close to her chest like that, but being hurt by Jack had changed her. Elliott thought she would always be a little more cautious in the future, more guarded. But he was glad it hadn't made her too afraid to try. That wouldn't have been the Marianne he knew

"I hope you make each other happy," he said.

Marianne smiled, her eyes lighting up.

Elliott laughed and kissed the top of her head.

"But you can't tell Mom," Marianne cautioned him. "Deanna thinks she's going to freak out because of the age thing."

"*Our* mom? She thinks *our* mom would freak out? She's met our mom, right?"

"She worries. It's sweet."

From over by the grill, Deanna was watching them, and yeah, that was worry creasing her brow and tugging her mouth down. Elliott had the impression she knew exactly what secrets Marianne was spilling.

He smiled at her, and she looked startled, and then embarrassed, and then she quickly turned her back to them.

Marianne stole a sip of his wine. "I've been looking at college courses."

"Yeah?"

"Yeah." She nodded. "I'm thinking of nursing. The nurses at the hospital were so good to me. And the ones here at the clinic, too."

"I think you'd be really good at that, Mar," Elliott told her. "I think you'd be amazing."

They fell silent as John, emboldened by more than a few glasses of wine, brought out his old acoustic guitar and strummed it a few times. Paula sat by him and watched fondly. Abby joined them.

"Ah," John said. "Remember this one, Abby? You taught me to play this one."

Elliott didn't recognize the tune until John began to sing and Abby joined in, then Paula, and he realized it was Leonard Cohen's "Dance Me to the End of Love." Elliott remembered his parents swaying together and singing it years and years before. He'd always found it somehow sad and beautiful at the same time, but his parents had smiled as they'd sung it, and they'd always been sure to end it with a kiss.

Elliott wanted that, one day.

He wanted someone who would kiss him when their song ended.

***

Tuesday was coupon day at the restaurant, and Elliott worked the lunchtime rush. Anyone who'd clipped the coupon out from the edge of the Barton Lake tourist map got half price on their second meal, and it was a trick the locals had wised up to long ago. Elliott wasn't sure any of the Tuesday crowd were tourists at all. Most of them came straight from the old people's home in Whitwell, and they were always super critical of the service, and of the food itself. And they were shitty tippers. Elliott hated Tuesdays, but he'd been taking as many shifts as he could in the two months since they'd gotten back from New York, and that included Tuesday lunchtimes. But there were a few regulars he liked and looked forward to seeing. Mrs. Ketteridge, who paid the tip with quarters. Mr. O'Brien: "Call me Bob." There were one or two others whose names he didn't know yet, but they were always polite and friendly.

Sometimes Elliott looked back over the past few months—his dad's death, coming to California, that entire fucking disaster that had been New York—and thought that maybe, at last, he was getting a handle on things. He had his routine. Marianne was healing. Abby was spending more and more time in the shop, and with her enthusiasm for all of that "hippie bullshit"—Greta's words—she was a better fit for the clientele than Elliott ever would be.

Greta was settling into school. She had friends now, an eclectic group of kids who were just as odd as she was. Elliott liked them.

Elliott finished his shift, shoved his apron in a plastic bag, and then headed for home.

It was a cold, wet day in Barton Lake. Elliott cut down the alley between the restaurant and the bookstore, and stepped into the laneway that ran behind Main Street. He avoided the worst of the puddles on the cracked asphalt by walking on the muddy verge where the wilted brown grass met the narrow road. It was easier to clean the mud off his shoes when he got home than have to dry them out entirely before his next shift.

He had a small life now. A small life in a small town, with small ambitions. It was enough. Elliott had never chased anything larger. Marianne was the dreamer, and Greta was the iconoclast. Elliott was the dependable one. The quiet one. The sensible one. And that was fine. That was enough.

It was enough.

A long legged bird stared at Elliott as he passed, its feathers fluffed up to protect it from the weather.

Elliott drew his coat tighter around him as he turned into the back yard of the apartment. He stopped short as he saw the figure sitting on the steps.

Blinked.

Ned Ferrars lifted his head and met his eyes.

Elliott stood there, frozen, as Ned pulled himself to his feet and then stepped down into the yard and toward him.

"What are you doing here?" Elliott blurted.

Ned hadn't changed. Fuck, of course he hadn't. It had been months, not years. Months since Elliott had seen him last that night at the Boathouse, when he'd been so cold toward him. Like they'd never kissed. Like they'd never done more than that either.

Ned's expression was pinched and anxious. "I, um, I came to see you."

"Why would you do that?"

Ned was a barely healed wound. Ned was scar tissue. Why would he come back here just to rip Elliott's skin open again? His skin. His heart. It wasn't fair that Elliott still wanted him. Wasn't fair how he couldn't bring himself to hate him.

It was stupid, what his heart wanted. What the hell did it know?

Ned looked startled. "I . . ."

He trailed off. Cold rain began to patter down, leaving dark spots on Ned's probably-expensive suede jacket. He didn't seem to notice the water beading on his shoulders. Elliott resisted the urge to reach out and brush the droplets off.

"Come upstairs," he said, digging his keys out of his pocket.

He climbed the steps, with Ned following.

The apartment was empty. Abby was downstairs working in the shop, Greta was still at school, and Marianne was probably over at Deanna's place.

Elliott shrugged his coat off and threw it onto the couch. Then he turned to Ned again, still hardly able to believe he was here. Ned was still standing anxiously just inside the doorway.

Elliott gestured toward the small table. "Do you want some tea?"

Ned shook his head. "No. No, thank you."

Perfect manners, like always. Which, on the scale of zero to cheating-on-his-fiancé didn't count for jack shit, right?

Elliott moved into the kitchen, filling the kettle and setting it on the stovetop. He suddenly wished they had something stronger than tea. He suspected he knew where Marianne's stash of weed was hidden, but maybe that was better saved for later. For the inevitable fallout of whatever the fuck this was.

He clattered around finding a clean mug.

"So," he said at last, turning back to where Ned was sitting at the table, hands held in his lap. "How's the family?"

"Um, good." Ned pressed his mouth into a line. Then he relaxed it again, and caught his lower lip between his teeth. He reached out for something on the table—the cracked little worry stone, Elliott saw—and fitted it into his palm. Rubbed his thumb over the same crack that Elliott did compulsively. "Good, thank you."

Elliott leaned against the counter and folded his arms over his chest. "How's your mother?"

Ned flinched a little at that. "She's well."

"I hear you're not buying the land. I guess that was a wasted trip, right?"

Ned's brow creased. "Elliott, I—"

"And congratulations," Elliott said, his stomach twisting. He pulled his shoulders back so he didn't look like he was curling into himself.

The crease on Ned's forehead deepened into a furrow. "Um. I'm sorry?"

"Congratulations," Elliott said again. "On the wedding."

"The wedding?" Ned repeated slowly.

"I'm sure Francesca and your mother will come around eventually. Lucien's an incredible guy."

"Yes, he is." Ned tilted his head on an angle, as though he really wasn't following this conversation at all. He set the worry stone down again.

"I'm sure you'll be very happy together," Elliott said, fighting to keep the bitterness out of his voice. He turned back to the stovetop as the kettle began to whistle, and lifted it off the burner.

"Elliott," Ned said, his voice strained.

Elliott couldn't look at him.

"Elliott, Lucien and I aren't married."

Elliott dropped the kettle, leaping back as it hit the floor and boiling water flooded the floor. "Fuck!"

He heard Ned's chair being pushed back, and a moment later Ned was holding him from behind, fingers wrapped around Elliott's wrists as he tugged his hands up to check them. "Are you burned?"

Elliott's left hand was throbbing.

Ned pulled him over to the sink, turning the cold water on and shoving his hand under it.

Elliott stared dumbly at his hand. At Ned holding it under the water. He turned his head, his nose brushing Ned's cheek. Ned smelled like the sort of aftershave Elliott could probably never afford. "You got married. Paula said you got married."

"*Robert* got married," Ned said.

Elliott felt the breath rush out of him. "What?"

"It was Robert," Ned said. "It was Robert who got married."

"I didn't even know he was engaged," Elliott said numbly.

"He eloped. With, um, with Lucien."

Elliott spun around so quickly he almost elbowed Ned in the face. "*What*?"

Ned was still holding his wrist. "I was out of town when Francesca found out about Lucien. She went ballistic."

"Yeah," Elliott said. "She does that."

Ned grimaced. "Lucien called. He was frantic. So I sent Robert to go and talk to him. Calm him down." He shrugged, and shook his head. "I, um, I guess they really hit it off?"

"What." The word was too flat to be a question. Elliott shook his head. "Why would Lucien . . ."

"Because he's smarter than me." Ned gave a rueful smile. "Because he manned up before I did and figured out that neither of us deserved to just settle."

"But your *brother*?"

Ned grimaced. "Yeah. That's been kind of weird to deal with."

"Understatement of the year?"

Ned made a face. "Robert's avoiding me because he thinks I'm pissed, Francesca doesn't know which one of us to hate the most, and my mother booked herself into the most expensive spa she could find and is refusing to speak to any of us. The only one I'm actually still talking to is Lucien."

"That . . . that sounds like a really bad telenovela, to be honest.

Like the ones that are so bad you can't stop watching."

Ned huffed out a breath. "Thank you, though, for reducing my life to the level of a telenovela."

"My millionaire relatives threw me and my sisters out of our home without a penny," Elliott said. "I can judge you."

Ned's expression softened with a smile. "That's fair."

Elliott gazed at him for a moment. The air shifted around them. The silence grew more laden, and Elliott was aware not only of his hand throbbing a little where the water had scalded it, but also of the way that Ned was still holding his wrist, his thumb rubbing gently against his pulse point.

Elliott tilted his chin up. "Why are you here?" he whispered.

Ned held his gaze. "I'm here for you, Elliott."

Elliott swore his heart stopped beating.

And then Ned leaned in and kissed him.

CHAPTER 20

"Wait," Elliott said, tugging at Ned's hair to pull him back, and then leaning in for another quick kiss despite that. He smiled at his own vacillation, and broke the kiss. "Wait."

They stood, their faces close, their hands restlessly traveling. Elliott plucked at the back of Ned's suede jacket and then smoothed his palm down it. Was he really allowed to do this? Was he really allowed to touch? He shivered as Ned curled a hand around his hip and nudged him back against the counter.

"Wait," he said again, ducking his head to avoid the distraction of another kiss. "What about Lucien?"

"I'm not married to Lucien."

Elliott got a hand on his chest and pushed him gently so there was some space between them. "You don't just . . . you don't just get to say that. I need to know what it was."

Ned nodded. He raised a hand and lifted it to Elliott's temple, then smoothed his hair back. "It was four years ago. Lucien was . . ." His mouth quirked into a rueful smile. "He was a breath of fresh air. He didn't care that my name was on the building. He made me laugh."

Elliott could feel Ned's heart beating under the heel of his hand. "Did you love him?"

"I thought I did," Ned said, and then exhaled. "That's a cop out, isn't it? Yes, I did love him."

Elliott dropped his gaze.

"Lucien is . . ." Ned made a small sound of frustration. "He's fun and he's an extravert, and I thought that if I was with someone like that then *I* would be like that too. When I met him I thought that he was everything I wanted, and that being with him would make me different, *better*, but that's not how it works. I tried, but Lucien likes clubs, and dancing, and poetry slams, and the art scene, and meeting new people, and I . . . I *don't*." He shook his head helplessly. "I just want to stay in and read a good book."

Elliott huffed out a laugh, because staying in with a book sounded like his idea of heaven. "And Robert likes the same things as Lucien?"

The younger Ferrars brother had seemed so incredibly *bland*, but John had said he was the wild one.

"He actually does." Ned traced the edge of Elliott's ear with his thumb. When he spoke again, his voice was soft. "At times like this, people always say they're not the same people they were when they met. But Lucien and I are exactly the same people we were when we met, and that's the problem." He exhaled heavily. "That's probably a cop out too."

Probably.

But right now, in this moment, Elliott didn't care, because Ned wasn't engaged anymore. Ned wasn't anyone's, which meant that maybe there was a chance he could be Elliott's, and maybe that was a thing Elliott still wanted despite however much he'd tried to deny it. However much he'd tried to tamp those feelings down, to smother them until they were nothing and pretend they weren't the things that kept him from sleeping at night. Kept him staring at the ceiling, watching the strange patterns of light dancing there and hating himself for his fantasies of having Ned Ferrars in his life. He'd never thought it was possible.

"I thought . . ." Ned cleared his throat. "I thought what I had with Lucien was enough. I thought that's what it was all about. He was a good friend to me. He still is, I hope. I didn't know there was even the possibility of feeling something more than that. Not until I met you."

"You came here," Elliott said, his heart thumping, his tongue tripping over the words. "You came here and I tried—" He shook his head. "I thought I'd got it all wrong, what happened between us at Norland Park. I thought you didn't care."

"I did," Ned said, his voice strained. "But I couldn't, with Lucien . . ."

"But we already had." Elliott closed his eyes for a moment. "You cheated."

"I told myself that didn't count."

Elliott jutted out his chin. "It counts!"

"I know. I know it does." Ned cupped his hand to Elliott's face. Brushed his thumb along his jawbone and held his gaze. "I told myself what happened with you was an aberration, and it wouldn't happen again. And then when I came here, I realized how much of a lie that was. I *wanted* you, Elliott. I wanted you all over again."

A thrill ran through Elliott. The thrill of Ned wanting to possess him, and of wanting to possess Ned in return.

"Okay," he said, lifting the corner of his mouth in a wry smile.

Ned's brows drew together. "Okay?" he asked, sounding puzzled.

"Yes. It's okay. You want me, and we're not hurting Lucien, and it's okay." He curled his fingers behind Ned's neck and pressed their foreheads together. He breathed the same air Ned did. Lucien was happy. It didn't make it right, but nobody had to hurt. Not this time. Not in Elliott's story. "It's *okay*."

He felt the tension in the back of Ned's neck ease. His shoulders slumped, and he exhaled slowly.

"I want you," Ned said. "I want you in my life. That's what I came here to tell you. I want to get to know you. I want to make pancakes with you without a recipe. I want you to meet my mother—"

Elliott winced.

"Yeah." Ned flushed. "That's going to be a disaster. She'll hate you, but she hates everyone, so don't take it personally."

Elliott snorted.

Ned stole another quick kiss. "I want to spend time with you. I want to watch you paint."

"I'm a terrible painter," Elliott reminded him with a low laugh.

"I don't care." Ned pulled back a few inches and dug his phone out of the pocket of his pants. He unlocked the screen and scrolled through a couple of photographs. "This, um, this is my apartment. This is the living room."

He turned the phone so Elliott could see the photo.

A gorgeous living space, open and clean. And on the wall was one of the shittiest paintings Elliott had ever seen. Swathes of color with no structure at all. It was . . . what had he called it? Sophomoric and unsophisticated and messy, the sort of thing you'd buy in a dollar store, and Elliott couldn't stop the smile spreading over his face as he saw how it had pride of place in Ned's living room.

It was worse than he remembered, actually, the paint smeared and smudged from when Ned had pushed him up against the canvas, their dicks in their hands. Elliott could still remember picking flakes of paint out of his hair the next day, and he hated to think what other smears a black light would reveal.

"You kept my terrible painting."

"It's not terrible," Ned said, sliding his phone back into his pocket.

"It really is. But thank you."

Ned leaned in for a kiss: a soft, gentle kiss that felt like a promise.

It was the sort of kiss that belonged at the end of a story, at the end of a song.

It was the sort of kiss Elliott could have melted into, except the kitchen floor was covered in water from the dropped kettle, and if Elliott didn't clean it up, who the hell else would?

He went and grabbed a spare towel from the bathroom.

When he got back, Ned took it off him without a word and wiped the floor.

***

The most unexpected thing about Ned's reappearance in Barton Lake, Elliott thought later, was Abby's equanimity. Not only was she dying to ask exactly how all this had come about, but Elliott was also sure that the old Abby would have been itching to drag Ned into a hug, remind him that love was the most powerful force in the universe, and welcome him into the family, and wasn't everything *wonderful*?

Jack Willoughby hadn't just hurt Marianne though.

Abby was restrained. She asked after Ned's family, and held all her other questions behind the pointed, questioningly looks she threw at Elliott.

Ned being here wasn't a happy ending. It was a beginning, and for once Abby was mindful of Elliott's caution.

Marianne's delight was more uninhibited, but still subdued by her old standards. She hugged them both, showed Ned the cast she was wearing under her billowing patchwork skirt, and then retreated to her room to call Lucien and get all the details of his unexpected elopement with Robert Ferrars.

She stopped to squeeze Elliott's shoulder as she limped toward her room.

Ned's gaze tracked her. When she had closed the door behind herself, Ned turned to Elliott. His brow was creased. "Is Marianne okay? She seems different."

"It's been a rough few months." Elliott was surprised that Ned hadn't heard about what'd happened from Lucien. Then again, he and Lucien had probably had more on their minds than the Dashwoods the last time they spoke.

Abby made them tea, a soft noise of surprise escaping her when she spotted the dent in the kettle. Then she picked up her purse and announced she was going to get some groceries.

Elliott took the opportunity to learn the ways that Ned liked to be kissed. He was shameless and shy at the same time. Reckless and also reserved. He wasn't sure he knew who this person was that Ned was uncovering with each kiss, each smile. He felt unknown. He felt *new*, every hidden part of his soul revealed now. His throat, his belly, all the softest parts of him offered up trustingly to Ned, and nothing he could do except that hope Ned wouldn't tear him into pieces.

When he met Ned's gaze, though, he saw the same fears reflected there.

It would be okay, maybe.

"Hey," Greta said when she arrived home after school, as though Ned being here was no big deal. As though finding him sitting on the couch holding Elliott's hand was an everyday occurrence.

"Hey," Ned said.

Greta dumped her backpack on the floor and then stomped into the kitchen to raid the refrigerator.

"I finished *Assassination Classroom*," Ned told her.

Greta reappeared with a tub of yogurt.

"It's possibly the weirdest thing I've ever watched," Ned said. "Then I found *Sayonara, Zetsubou-Sensei*."

Greta raised her eyebrows. "What did you think of it?"

"I think that I never want to go to high school in Japan."

Greta smiled. An honest-to-god smile that lit up her entire expression. "I *know*, right?"

***

It was late when they pulled up on Pier Lane, at one of the picnic areas that dotted the lakeside. The night was bright and cold. The moonlight danced on the surface of the lake. The air smelled of pine.

Elliott stepped over the low barrier that separated the parking lot from the grass, and Ned followed him. They walked shoulder to shoulder down toward the lakeshore. Tiny waves lapped at the edge of the lake.

They sat on a picnic table that overlooked the water, their feet on the bench seat.

"It's beautiful here," Ned said at last. "So quiet."

Across the lake, the lights from the big houses glittered.

"Not beautiful enough for one of your hotels though, huh?" Elliott teased.

"The numbers didn't work out." Ned shrugged. "It's nice, but it's not Lake Tahoe, you know?"

"I guess." Elliott reached out and curled his fingers through Ned's. "There's a lot we need to figure out."

If Francesca had been pissed about Lucien, she was going to be apoplectic about Elliott. Poor John would probably bear the brunt of that for having the temerity to be related to Elliott in the first place, and compounding that sin by never having successfully severed Abby and her children from his life. She probably figured she'd finally gotten rid of them, only to have Elliott pop up again attached like a tick to Ned.

So that was something to look forward to.

There was distance too. Ned lived and worked out of New York, and Elliott lived in Barton Lake. That seemed like an added stressor to a thing that was still too new and fragile to bend under pressure instead of breaking.

There was money, too. When the hell was money not an issue? Ned had money. Capital-m Money. And Elliott had seventeen dollars in his wallet. That seemed like it would be complicated.

"There's a lot that could go wrong," Elliott said.

Ned squeezed his hand. "I think there's a lot that could go right, though."

"Yeah," Elliott said softly, warmth filling him.

And that was love, wasn't it?

Maybe it wasn't chemistry, or fate, or the adventure of a lifetime. Maybe love was, at its simplest, optimism. Maybe love was choosing to believe that it would all work out in the end.

Elliott looked across the lake at the big houses.

Once, over twenty years ago, a college student had knocked on a door somewhere over there and announced she was there for the nanny job. And two lives had collided over that summer. They took a chance. They made a choice. They weren't blameless. They were selfish, maybe. Their love came at a cost to the people around them. It hadn't been free of consequences.

But they'd danced together, right up until the end.

And if that was selfish, then maybe Elliott was selfish too. He wanted that. He wanted love. He wanted to hold onto it and never let it go.

That was his father's legacy, maybe. Not the art, not his background or the Family infighting, but his love for Abby. He'd shown Elliott what love could cost. He'd shown him that it was a choice he was allowed to make.

And here, under the moonlight, Elliott made that choice.

"What's your favorite song?" he asked Ned, raising their clasped hands to his mouth so he could press his lips to their fingers.

"What?" Ned smiled. "I don't know. Is it important?"

"Mmm." Elliott leaned forward. He closed his eyes as they kissed. "If we don't have a favorite song, what are we going to dance to late at night?"

Ned laughed. His breath was warm against Elliott's face. "I guess we'd better think of one."

"Yeah," Elliott said, his chest tight with happiness. "I guess we should."

Everything else could wait until tomorrow.

Dear Reader,

Thank you for reading Lisa Henry's *The California Dashwoods*!

We know your time is precious and you have many, many entertainment options, so it means a lot that you've chosen to spend your time reading. We really hope you enjoyed it.

We'd be honored if you'd consider posting a review—good or bad—on sites like **Amazon, Barnes & Noble, Kobo, Goodreads, Twitter, Facebook, Tumblr,** and your blog or website. We'd also be honored if you told your friends and family about this book. Word of mouth is a book's lifeblood!

For more information on upcoming releases, author interviews, blog tours, contests, giveaways, and more, please sign up for our weekly, spam-free newsletter and visit us around the web:

Newsletter: tinyurl.com/RiptideSignup
Twitter: twitter.com/RiptideBooks
Facebook: facebook.com/RiptidePublishing
Goodreads: tinyurl.com/RiptideOnGoodreads
Tumblr: riptidepublishing.tumblr.com

Thank you so much for Reading the Rainbow!

RiptidePublishing.com

Also by Lisa Henry

Emergency Services series
Two Man Station
Lights and Sirens (coming
soon)

Adulting 101
Sweetwater
He Is Worthy
The Island
Tribute
One Perfect Night
Fallout, with M. Caspian
Fall on Your Knees (part of the
Rated: XXXmas anthology)

With J.A. Rock
When All the World Sleeps
Another Man's Treasure

*Playing the Fool series,
with J.A. Rock*
The Two Gentlemen of Altona
The Merchant of Death
Tempest

With Heidi Belleau
Tin Man
Bliss
King of Dublin
The Harder They Fall

Writing as Cari Waites
Stealing Innocents

About the Author

Lisa likes to tell stories, mostly with hot guys and happily ever afters.

Lisa lives in tropical North Queensland, Australia. She doesn't know why, because she hates the heat, but she suspects she's too lazy to move. She spends half her time slaving away as a government minion, and the other half plotting her escape.

She attended university at sixteen, not because she was a child prodigy or anything, but because of a mix-up between international school systems early in life. She studied History and English, neither of them very thoroughly.

She shares her house with too many cats, a green tree frog that swims in the toilet, and as many possums as can break in every night. This is not how she imagined life as a grown-up.

You can email me at lisahenryonline@gmail.com
Or check out my website at lisahenryonline.com
Got Twitter? Follow me at twitter.com/LisaHenryOnline
Hanging out on Goodreads? So am I: Lisa Henry
Facebook: facebook.com/lisa.henry.1441

Enjoy more stories like *The California Dashwoods* at RiptidePublishing.com!

Loud and Clear

Learning to communicate could be their biggest challenge.

ISBN: 978-1-62649-434-3

How the Cookie Crumbles

He wants nothing more than to prove he's changed.

ISBN: 978-1-62649-389-6